SILENT NIGHT

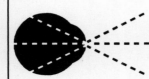

This Large Print Book carries the
Seal of Approval of N.A.V.H.

SILENT NIGHT

A SPENSER HOLIDAY NOVEL

ROBERT B. PARKER
WITH HELEN BRANN

THORNDIKE PRESS

A part of Gale, Cengage Learning

GALE
CENGAGE Learning®

Detroit • New York • San Francisco • New Haven, Conn • Waterville, Maine • London

GALE
CENGAGE Learning·

LIBRARY OF CONGRESS CATALOGING-IN-PUBLICATION DATA

Parker, Robert B., 1932-2010.
  Silent night : a Spenser Holiday novel / by Robert B. Parker with Helen Brann. — Large print edition.
    pages ; cm. — (A Spenser novel) (Thorndike Press large print core)
  ISBN 978-1-4104-6431-6 (hardcover) — ISBN 1-4104-6431-8 (hardcover) 1. Spenser (Fictitious character)—Fiction. 2. Private investigators—Massachusetts—Boston—Fiction. 3. Boston (Mass.)—Fiction. 4. Large type books. I. Brann, Helen. II. Title.
PS3566.A686S56 2013b
813'.54—dc23   2013036705

Published in 2013 by arrangement with G. P. Putnam's Sons, a member of Penguin Group (USA) LLC, a Penguin Random House Company

Printed in the United States of America
1 2 3 4 5 6 7 17 16 15 14 13

Joan:
Every Christmas gift I cherished
came nicely wrapped as you.

1

Susan and I walked from my place up to Newbury Street on a sunny Saturday morning. The snow from the night before had stopped falling. There wasn't much traffic, mostly cabs and an occasional noisy snowplow. It was two weeks before Christmas. A Salvation Army worker in full uniform was ringing a bell beside a tripod bucket at the corner of Boylston and Berkeley.

"I'm glad we don't exchange presents anymore," I said.

"Me too," Susan said. "Have you canceled your account at Victoria's Secret?"

"Reluctantly. But they still send me the catalog."

"You could probably have your name removed from the list," Susan said.

"Sure."

She smiled.

We went into a women's boutique, where the staff seemed to know Susan. I found a chair designed for a woman who weighed 108 pounds. I resumed my lifelong comparative study of the female form. Susan had opened a nearly insurmountable lead. That was no reason not to see who might be runner-up. Or in the top ten. After about forty minutes we left. Susan had bought what she referred to as a "lovely little top." And several small packages in a shopping bag decorated with a large Santa Claus.

"I didn't think Jews did Christmas shopping," I said.

"More often we do Christmas selling. You do realize there's a group of us at Harvard who gather every year and drink wine and exchange one gift each."

"Any men in this group?"

"No."

"Sounds like a fun crowd. A gathering of Harvard women."

"It can get a little fustian at times," Susan said. "But I like these women, and there's something sort of nice about a girls' night out."

"Sort of like Hawk and me at the fights?"

"Sort of."

We turned the corner and into the bar door of the Taj Boston, formerly the Ritz, for a libation at the table we liked overlooking the Garden.

"I'll have a glass of Edna Valley chardonnay," Susan said to the waiter.

"Johnnie Walker Blue, soda, high-ball," I said.

Susan smiled at me. "I like your Christmas spirit."

"And I like yours."

Susan sipped her wine. "Why do you suppose a grown woman, a doctor, a therapist at that, feels at Christmastime the same sense of excitement and anticipation she did when she was just a girl?"

"Perhaps we'll need to discuss this later," I said, lifting my glass.

"I do hope so," Susan said, and raised her glass to me. "At length."

2

I stood at my office window and looked out at the snow falling quietly onto the Back Bay and muffling the gleam of the Christmas lighting in the store windows. The snow had come often this year.

"Fa, la, la," I said.

Pearl raised her head. She was with me on a take-your-dog-to-work day, which she spent, as she often did, on the couch in my office. I looked at her.

"La, la," I said.

She didn't know what I was talking about, but she was used to that. She could also sense that whatever it was, it had no connection to food. So she put her head back down on her paws and watched me in silent resignation.

I liked the myth elements of Christmas. The way in which its origins reach back far beyond Jesus, to the rituals of people unknown to us. The celebration of the winter solstice. The coming of light in the darkest time. And with it the promise of spring to come and beginning again. I liked it better than Rudolph the Red-Nosed Reindeer.

I went to my desk and sat down.

"Actually," I said to Pearl, "I've had bad colds I liked better than

Rudolph the Red-Nosed Reindeer."

I sensed movement in her look. Then she lost interest and snapped her head toward the door and made a low growl. Hospitality dog.

The door opened and a kid came in.

He looked at Pearl and said, "That dog going to bite me?"

"Not," I said, "unless you attack me."

"Attack you?"

"Uh-huh."

"For crissake, I'm a fucking kid."

"I guessed that. Have a seat."

Still watching Pearl, the kid sat down opposite my desk. His face was pointy and his eyes were close. He was wearing gray sweatpants that were too long for him. The bottoms of the pant legs were torn and ragged where the heel of his sneakers had repeatedly caught in them. His jacket was a threadbare navy peacoat, also too big, with the sleeves turned back. Under it was a gray hoodie. His baseball cap had a flat brim, and he wore it level and straight under the hood.

"How old are you?"

"Eleven, I think."

"You think?"

"Yeah. I was there, but I don't remember it, you know."

"What about your parents? You know them?"

"My old lady was a drunk. I don't think she knew who my old man was."

"She the one who raised you?"

"Awhile," the kid said. "Then she didn't."

"Run off?"

"Wherever she went, she went."

"So who raised you?"

"The orphanage."

"How was that?"

"Sucked," the kid said. "You wanna hear why I come to see you?"

"I do."

"I live in a place."

"Where," I said.

He made a looping gesture with his right hand.

"Around," he said.

"Nice neighborhood."

The kid frowned at me. He was so street-worn and tough-talking and life-weary that I forgot he was only eleven. Irony is not the long suit of eleven-year-olds.

"You don't know where I live," he said.

"No," I said. "I was just making a little joke."

"Ain't funny."

"No," I said. "Probably not. What's your name?"

"Slide."

"Last name?"

"Slide," he said.

I nodded.

"What do you want me to do for you?"

"I want you to talk with Jackie," Slide said.

"Who's Jackie?" I said.

"Jackie asked me to come here

and deliver his message. He needs to see you."

"What does he want to talk to me about?"

"He'll tell you."

"Why me?"

"He seen you on the TV."

"Why didn't Jackie come?" I said.

"He sent me. He wanted to know if you would see him," Slide said.

"How long have you known Jackie?"

"A few weeks," he said.

I nodded. "And before that?"

He shuffled uncomfortably in the chair. "Did odd jobs. Slept where I could. The Y. You know."

"Uh-huh," I said.

"Will you see Jackie?"

I took a card out of the middle

drawer of my desk and gave it to him.

"You or Jackie call me when you're ready," I said.

"Okay," he said.

The kid took the card and put it in the side pocket of his pants without looking at it. Then he stood up and looked at me and didn't say anything and turned and went out.

I went to my window and watched him walk through the snow, his shoulders hunched, hands in his pockets, staying close to the walls of buildings, until he turned the corner onto Boylston Street and disappeared in the direction of the Public Garden.

3

We were at my place. I was making supper. Susan was at my kitchen counter. Pearl had stretched out the length of the sofa, longer than one would think possible for a seventy-five-pound dog.

"Tell me more about this boy who came to see you," Susan said.

"His name is Slide, he's eleven, and he lives with someone named Jackie in a place whose location is unknown."

"That's all?" she said.

I mixed bread crumbs and pignolis with a little olive oil and began to toast them in a fry pan on low.

"Except he's terrified of his own shadow." I stirred the contents of the pan, which were beginning to brown.

"And who is Jackie?" she said.

"Not much to go on," I said.

I took the fry pan off the fire and emptied the toasted crumbs and pignolis into a bowl. I took an Amstel Light out of the refrigerator and opened it. I poured it into a tall glass. After a swallow, I said, "If you didn't know, how old would you think you were?"

"Twenty-eight," Susan said.

"Plausible," I said. "But you're far too smart to be only twenty-eight."

"I try to conceal that."

"You fail."

"I wonder why Jackie sent a boy instead of coming himself," Susan said. I watched her sip her wine. After an hour, the glass was still half full. "You'll talk with Jackie?"

"If he gets in touch," I said.

"What if it's something illegal," Susan said.

"There's illegal and illegal," I said. "I make part of my living from that fact."

Susan nodded.

I turned up the heat under the pot of water on the stove and put some whole-wheat linguine in it and set my timer. I sat on a bar stool opposite Susan, who took another sip and said, "Let me see if

I have this right. Slide is sent by this guy named Jackie, who may or may not ever appear. And although you don't fully grasp the situation, something about Slide has got you interested in helping him, whether Jackie's activities are legal or not."

"Slide's eleven going on thirty. So far life hasn't been full of good times for him. He's afraid. Somewhere along the line he got scared, real bad. Of who, or what?"

"And maybe Jackie is the key to figuring out what's happening," Susan said.

The timer went off and I went over and drained the linguine. "Whatever Jackie turns out to be, or whether or not he shows up, Slide is definitely in some kind of

23

trouble."

"Slide is a convenient cover for Jackie to hide whatever he's up to," Susan said. "And since he didn't come himself, it would appear that at the very least Slide is being used."

"A Boston version of Oliver Twist," I said. I plated the pasta and brought the plates over to the counter.

"There wasn't much Charles Dickens in our house," Susan said.

"That's because you spent your time reading the diaries of Sigmund Freud." I picked up my fork. "A match made in heaven."

"So deep down, we're really just a couple of Victorians?" she said.

"Maybe not. Just that we were

educated early in the analysis of motivation," I said. "Dickens, Freud, they're all alike in the dark."

Susan laughed. "Mrs. Freud might disagree with you on that."

It was quiet for a moment. Then Susan said, "Have you given any thought to how we should spend Christmas?"

"Only that we should be together." I glanced over at the softly snoring Pearl. "With Pearl, of course. Hawk, too. Maybe ask Paul if he can join us."

"We'll do it at my place. You know how I love to set a nice table for Christmas."

"A beautiful paradox," I said. "But anywhere you are, it's Christmas to me."

4

The next morning I met Hawk at the Harbor Health Club. Hawk was doing combinations on the heavy bag and I was hitting the double-end jeeter bag with my left hand. Hawk didn't break a sweat. After ten minutes I was sodden and winded.

"You do any more damage to that bag, we'll have to get Henry a new one for Christmas," I said.

"Fuck Christmas," he said.

"Wow," I said. "And people say

you're not sentimental. You still bitter that Santa Claus is a white man?"

Hawk began to hit the bag alternately with both hands.

"Whole holiday be a white man's scam. All those rich honkies running in and out of stores like they might miss buying the last Rolls on the floor. Bentley's beneath them." He shifted his feet a little and started hitting the heavy bag with his left hand.

"This from a guy who drives a Jaguar," I said. "I would think you'd appreciate a nice Rolls."

"Jag be subtle elegance, babe. Rolls just someone tryin' too hard to impress people who don't know better. That's Christmas."

"Well, Ebenezer, you had better work on your holiday spirit, or Susan's going to rescind her invitation to Christmas dinner."

Hawk stopped, lightly tapped the bag with his left hand, and looked at me.

"Christmas dinner? At Susan's?"

I nodded. "We could call it a Kwanzaa dinner, if that would improve your mood."

Hawk ignored me. "Just the three of us?"

"And Pearl," I said.

"How about Paul?"

Paul Giacomin had spent several Christmases with Susan and me in the years since I had helped liberate him from his parents.

"Susan called — Paul will be at

28

his in-laws' this Christmas. We may visit him in New York after the New Year."

"So just us? And Pearl?"

I nodded. "Unless there's someone special you'd like to invite."

"No one special at the moment." Hawk grinned. " 'Course, it ain't Christmas yet."

"So can I let Susan know you'll be cruising by in the Jag to join us?"

"Tell Susan I'm looking forward to it."

"I can feel her blushing already," I said.

Hawk went back to pummeling the heavy bag.

"Dinner better be at Susan's house, though. Wouldn't park my car in your neighborhood, even if it is just a Jag."

After we wound down, we walked to the South Street Diner at Kneeland Street. Hawk ordered a coffee with skim milk and two Equals. No donut. I ordered a coffee and two corn muffins. Between the first and second muffin, I told him about Slide. "He's the most terrified kid trying not to show it I've ever seen."

"I knew a boy like that once," Hawk said.

"You." I said it without thinking, knowing I was right.

Hawk looked at me. To the world, Hawk appeared impassive and impenetrable. And mostly, he was. I had been around him long enough, though, that I could recognize subtle changes. Things most people didn't see, or didn't notice. But I knew Hawk — to the extent anyone could know him — better than most people did. And now it was Christmas, a time for revelations. Maybe Susan could explain it to me. Perhaps it was a vestige of our need to huddle by the cave fire together and tell stories, to ward off the darkness outside.

Hawk stirred his coffee. I watched the people come and go by the cash register, bundled up against the eighteen-degree weather.

"When I was about Slide's age, I hit the streets. The winter was always the worst. I got money to eat any way I could." Hawk looked at me. "Any way."

"This kid is scared. I don't see you being scared."

Hawk took a sip of his coffee. He placed the cup back down on the saucer and leveled his gaze at me.

"All kids scared one time or other. You on your own, you learn how to take care of yourself."

I nodded. "You survive long enough, you learn not to be afraid."

"Or you don't survive, and it don't matter."

Hawk drained the rest of his coffee, then counted out his tip.

"You have help?"

Hawk stood up and slid into his parka.

"Lotta help, 'long the way," he said. He paused. "One day I meet a cocktail waitress and she help me grow up real fast. I was sixteen and she was twenty." He grinned. "Haven't been scared since."

5

While I wasn't feeling particularly holly jolly about Christmas, I was quite interested in Christmas dinner. Sometimes we went out, and sometimes we stayed home, where I cooked and Susan stayed out of the way. I had been pondering wild boar. While I toyed with the idea of hunting it myself, I opted for a more refined approach. I explored the exotic game at Savenor's on Charles Street. Then I drove out to Newton to inspect the offerings at

John Dewar. Just in case I encountered a wild boar on the way to the suburbs, I took my gun.

Maybe turducken . . .

When I got back to my office, waiting outside the door was a smooth, strapping guy with a lot of dark curly hair and the open professional smile of a television star. He was wearing an ill-fitting blue blazer over a collarless black shirt and gray slacks. His clothes had the worn and rumpled look of a thrift store sale.

He smiled. "My name's Jackie. I was wondering if I could talk with you."

"Come in," I said, and unlocked the door.

I motioned him into the office. He stood next to one of the guest chairs until I had made my way around the desk. I sat. He sat. I tented my hands, rested my chin on my fingertips, and waited. The room grew quiet enough for me to hear the traffic noise from the street below. The steam radiator hissed.

"First thing," Jackie said finally. "My name is Joachim Lorenzo Alvarez."

"You obviously know mine."

"I do," Jackie said.

"So you know my name and what I do," I said.

"And you only know my name?" Jackie said.

"Exactly," I said.

"How much has Slide told you?"

"Not much."

"I run an organization called Street Business," Jackie said. "I give kids a place to live. I get jobs for them."

I waited.

"Street Business gives a home and work and structure to kids who need them," Jackie said. "We provide an opportunity for runaways, those abandoned by their families or who are alone because of circumstances over which they have no control."

"Excuse me, Jackie," I said. "But you sound like you're reading from a brochure. You help kids. I get that. Where do you find the kids you help?"

Jackie seemed to relax a bit. He

took a deep breath and gave a slight wave of his left hand. "Mostly, the kids find me. Word-of-mouth referrals. One kid tells another, that kind of thing. Sometimes they just turn up on my doorstep, who knows from where? Especially when it's cold out." He smiled at me. "My brother Juan has a large estate in Weston, and he sometimes sends me the children of the Mexican immigrants who work for him. They need to earn pocket money and learn English. Others are referred to me by those who are aware of my services. Kids just out of juvenile detention. Nowhere to go. That sort of thing. Their parents have kicked them out."

"Are you licensed?'

He looked down at his hands. "No," he said. "Not at this time."

I leaned back in my chair and contemplated what I was hearing. An unlicensed home for wayward kids. I considered the types of work a place like that would have kids do, and didn't like any of them. And how would he avoid getting caught by the cops, running an unlicensed business? Probably not a client I'd be highlighting on my website. If I had a website.

"Where does your financing come from?" I said.

"We'll take any help we can get. I take a percentage of what the kids make to help run the place, but it isn't enough by a long shot. My older brother Juan is our main support."

"Your brother has that kind of money?"

Jackie flashed a brief smile. "Please don't let my stylish clothing fool you, Mr. Spenser. I am not a wealthy man, but my brother is. He is a successful businessman with many interests."

"He's in Boston?"

Jackie brightened. "Yes. His office is here in town, in the Financial District."

"And why do you and your brother do this?"

"I started Street Business to help others avoid the mistakes I have made. My family came over from Puerto Rico and settled in Lawrence, where there's a big immigrant community. Our mother still lives there. I am not proud of this, but I fell in with gangs early. Juan never did. He left Lawrence as soon as he graduated from high school, traveled to Mexico and South America, came back a businessman. He is generous with his wealth, in the community and with his family. He got me out of the gang life and gave me a job. And when I told him I wanted to start Street Business, he bought me the house we use and gave me enough funds to get started."

"And when you run low, he helps you out?" I said.

"Yes."

"And what do you do about the law? Does your brother help you out with the being-unlicensed part, too?"

"Yes," Jackie said. "Juan has many friends in high places."

"What kinds of jobs do the kids do?" I said.

"A couple of Juan's guys live with us, and they help find them jobs. Bike messengers. Some are busboys. They can do the kinds of things in restaurants that aren't unionized. In the summer they mow lawns, do yard work, that kind of thing. You'd be surprised. We have some good mechanics and apprentice carpenters. People don't ask too many questions, if a sixteen-year-old kid is a good worker."

"And some are messengers, like

Slide," I said.

Jackie gave a little laugh that sounded like a hiccup.

"Yes, like Slide. When I can keep him from running back to Carmen."

"Who is Carmen?" I said.

"She's Juan's girlfriend. She lives on his estate out in Weston. Slide turned up out there a week or so ago. Carmen told me he looked like he had been hitchhiking for a while. His last ride must have dumped him off on the Weston highway. I guess he could see my brother's big red barn from the road and decided to sleep there, where he could stay warm. She found him in the morning up in the hayloft. After a few days, Carmen sent him to me to see if he could be useful running errands. But he's so attached to her, he keeps hopping a bus or hitchhiking back to Weston."

"Maybe he just prefers fresh air over Times Square," I said, "like on *Green Acres.*"

"What?" Jackie frowned.

"Nothing. So what problem do you have that you need me for?"

Jackie leaned forward and his voice dropped. "The property that Juan gave me? Where we both live and work? People are trying to make us get out."

"By means that require me, not a lawyer?" I said.

"Yes."

"And no cops?"

"That is correct," Jackie said.

"Because you aren't legal?"

"Yes," Jackie said. "We are not strictly legal. We are, as you noted, unlicensed. Some of the kids are underage and don't have any working papers. And some, as I mentioned, are illegal immigrants from Mexico."

"Who's trying to drive you out?"

"I'm not sure. It could be a street gang. Or the church. There is a local parish that is looking for property so they can expand. They want to build low-income housing and a school. Juan owns some other houses in the block where he puts his employees. At one time, the church wanted to buy us all out, but we wouldn't sell. Whoever it is, they take the kids' money and sometimes rough them up. A couple of the boys have been hurt, and plenty of them are frightened."

"If your brother Juan is so rich, why can't he find out who's trying to get rid of you and then do something about it?" I said.

"Juan supports us financially, but he keeps his distance from Street Business. It could have a negative impact on his business and social interests in Boston."

"And what exactly are Juan's business interests?" I said.

Jackie smiled at me as though I should know. "My brother has a very successful import/export business with offices all over the world. Alvarez Worldwide Limited. Since I am not a businessman, I do not pretend to understand all the ins and outs of what he does, but I do know he is very rich and powerful. Most of his business is between Mexico and the States, and he travels a great deal between the two."

"And what do you want me to do for you?"

"Find out who's trying to get rid of us and make them stop."

I nodded.

"Are you thinking about paying me?" I said.

"We will pay you what we can."

"Were you thinking about when?" I said.

"We will pay you when we can," he said.

"Gee," I said, "do you have the

same deal with the electric company?"

Jackie straightened in his chair and looked at me evenly.

"Mr. Spenser, it is not easy for me to ask for help. I am trying to do good in the community. I am being opposed by unknown forces that I cannot myself combat. I am told you are good at this. I am not. I tell you I will pay you what I can when I can. I am a man of my word, but that is the best I can offer. Will you help us, please?"

I leaned back in my chair and thought about my other cases. That didn't take long. I had no other cases. Crime in Boston had apparently taken an early holiday. Then I thought about the earnest man sitting in front of me, pleading for my help. I thought about Slide, a frightened kid trying desperately not to show fear. And I tried to imagine Hawk when he was Slide's age, living on the streets and learning to survive.

"Yes," I said. "I will help you."

After Jackie had gone, I phoned Hawk. I asked him to look into the background of Juan Alvarez and find out everything he could. I told him that I had agreed to help his younger brother, Jackie. I filled in the details and hoped for more to come.

6

We didn't need an excuse, but Hawk and I had arranged to meet at Jake Wirth's for a pre-Christmas lunch.

A waitress came by to take our orders. She was young and blond and wearing a green-and-white outfit that fell somewhere between a Hansel and Gretel costume and a cheerleader's uniform. Her short skirt revealed long, tan legs of the type you seldom see in Boston in the winter, the kind that make you yearn for spring.

In keeping with the season, I ordered a Sam Adams Winter Lager and a Jake's Burger with Russian dressing. Hawk ordered a Paulaner Hefeweizen and the Jaegerschnitzel.

Hawk shook his head. "Come to a place like this and order an American beer. Shame you aren't more adventurous."

"Just supporting local industry, and showing a little civic pride." I hoisted my mug. "Sam Adams, Brewer and Patriot."

Hawk snorted. "Stuff's brewed in Ohio. You just afraid of ordering anything you can't pronounce."

"And while you're showing off your command of German, I can

order two of these before you can say 'Hefeweizen.' "

A Muzak version of "Rudolph, the Red-Nosed Reindeer" infiltrated the din of lunchtime conversation. It was not a song that improved with repeated listening, though the Sam Adams helped.

Hawk looked up as his plate of veal was set in front of him. "Any progress finding out who's trying to get rid of Jackie's business?" He tucked his napkin into the open collar of his light green silk shirt.

My burger arrived, and I took a bite. "Jackie doesn't know who's behind it. He seems to think it may be the church looking to expand."

"Don't it seem odd to you that the church would be roughing up boys to scare this Alvarez into selling his property to them?"

"Forget about the punch line that's buried in there somewhere," I said. "You're right. It's more than odd. The church has plenty of money. And I doubt they'd need to resort to thuggery."

"I asked around about Juan Alvarez, and most everybody say the same thing. He's part of the Puerto Rican section of Lawrence that immigrated early part of last century. Some of them did well. Got an education. Became lawyers, bankers, and such. Some joined gangs and started a kind of Puerto Rican mafia. Juan chose the first path. He's something of a mystery man. He left town; nobody seems to know where he went, but he came back rich. Now he's Mr. Philanthropy in Boston. Very popular. Connected politically. Only one guy say something a little different," Hawk said.

I waited while Hawk forked some spaetzle.

"He says that Alvarez's been wanted by the Feds for years, but they can't pin anything on him. Suspect he be head of one of the biggest drug cartels coming out of Mexico. He just slippery."

Hawk's attention returned to his plate.

"He wouldn't be the first rich guy to use payoffs to politicians and contributions to charities to run circles around the Feds. They usually get caught on some trivial tax misdemeanor. Your guy a reliable source?" I said.

"No. Snitch done plenty of jail time. But no reason to lie to me, either. Gave him a fifty. Only 'cause it's Christmas. Otherwise, it would have been twenty."

"Good to hear you've embraced the holiday spirit," I said. "But that doesn't really explain how a poor kid from Lawrence rockets to wealth and prestige in Boston. He reinvents himself somehow, the old-fashioned American way, and we don't know how. Or why anyone would want to wreck his younger brother's enterprise, in this case Street Business, which seems to help young homeless boys get jobs and maybe even some self-respect. Besides getting the sense that this Juan Alvarez is a bit of a cipher, we don't really know diddly-squat."

"So where we start?"

"We?"

"Yeah," Hawk said. "Fair to say I'm a little curious about this Street Business. If it's legit, seem a shame for it to be shut down."

"And if it's not legit?"

"Like to shut it down personally," Hawk said.

I signaled our waitress for the check. I wasn't in a rush. But I wanted to admire her legs one more time before we left. It would be a long time until spring.

"Okay," I said. "Perhaps it's the

moment for some quiet contempla-
tion. Let's go to church."

7

Three blocks North of the harbor stood St. Bartholomew the Apostle Catholic Church, known locally as St. Bart's. We walked briskly from the car. The wind off the water was icy.

Outside St. Bart's gray granite walls in the ugly small yard was a Christmas crèche depicting the birth of Christ, with Mary and Joseph and the three Wise Men in attendance. When we entered we could hear the sweet, high-pitched boys' choir rehearsing Handel's Messiah in the back of the church. A burly, youngish man in a black suit and Roman collar approached us. He smiled. "May I help you?"

"I'm a private investigator. My name is Spenser. And this is Hawk," I said.

Hawk nodded at the priest.

"May we have five minutes of your time?" I said.

"Of course. I'm Father Ahearn. Please, follow me." He led us to a small office off the sacristy, then waved his arm in the direction of two guest chairs before sitting down behind a weathered wood desk.

"We were wondering if you know anything about the house on Curtis Street owned by a man named Alvarez. It's used for a place called Street Business."

"I know the property," Father Ahearn said, "but I can't say I know much about Street Business." He poured us each coffee from a carafe on a side table and passed around a plate of Christmas cookies. They looked homemade, stars and trees covered with red and green sprinkles. I took one of each.

"We understand that somebody out there would prefer that Street Business be gone," I said.

Father Ahearn smiled slightly. "Well, I might fall into that category," he said.

I nodded in what I hoped was an encouraging manner. Rule Number

17 of Effective Investigating: Keep them talking.

"I mean no disrespect to Street Business, and I mean them no harm, you understand. It's just that we have been looking to expand our ministry, and are looking for space to build low-income housing and a new elementary school."

"And Street Business stands in the way of your plans?"

Father Ahearn shook his head. "No, not exactly. We had looked into purchasing several of the houses on that block of Curtis Street, including the Street Business building. There aren't many options for expansion in the neighborhood. That location would suit our purposes nicely, and the buildings are in such a dilapidated condition that we thought the owners might be interested in selling. They appear to be sparsely and infrequently occupied. And, frankly, given the condition of the houses, we thought they might be available at an attractive price. We started by trying to approach the owners directly without intermediaries, feeling that often this is the best way to get things done. Right away we realized it was going to be difficult to find out exactly who the real owners were."

"And how did you proceed?" I said.

He sighed. "Alas, when we tracked down the various owners, none of them appeared interested in selling. The properties each have different owners, various realty trusts and so forth, but according to our lawyers they are all ultimately owned in one fashion or another by a single family, named Alvarez." Father Ahearn stopped and sipped his coffee. Hawk sat straight and motionless in the chair beside me.

"So why not go straight to Alvarez?" I said.

The priest shrugged. "We've decided to look elsewhere. There are other locations in Boston that will be satisfactory for our needs, just not as convenient."

"I appreciate your subtlety, Father, but I'm just not that smart. How come you backed off Alvarez?"

Father Ahearn chuckled and almost spilled his coffee. Hawk shifted slightly in his chair.

"You strike me as quite astute, Mr. Spenser. Of course, the first thing we did was to approach one of the members of the Alvarez family," Father Ahearn said. "Juan Alvarez, the family patriarch, is a generous benefactor to the parish, and to the Archbishop's Annual Appeal. We would never try to strong-arm him or his family. It would be ungracious, not to mention foolish. On the other hand, Mr. Alvarez was the obvious person for the church to approach, and we did. For whatever reason, he has no interest in selling any of his properties on Curtis Street. And for that reason alone, we had to look elsewhere."

"Do you have any idea who might have a reason to try to force Street Business out of the neighborhood? Somebody who doesn't care about the Annual Appeal?"

He shook his head. "No, I'm afraid I can't help you. This can be a tough neighborhood, which is why we are trying to expand our ministry here, to bring peace and civility through our work. There is crime, and gang tensions flare up from time to time. But I have not heard of any threats or problems with Street Business specifically."

Hawk and I stood up, and Father Ahearn walked us back through the church. "Beautiful, isn't it?" he said as the boys' voices filled the nave. He shook our hands at the door. "Thank you for stopping by."

As we went down the long stone steps, Father Ahearn called out, "Merry Christmas!"

I returned the greeting. Hawk was silent.

We sat in my car and looked at the church.

"Do you believe him?" I asked Hawk.

"Been a long time since I believed anything from a priest," said Hawk, "especially concerning young boys."

"Not all priests, Hawk," I said. "Not even most priests. Most are trying to do good things, in places just like this and worse."

"Yeah," he said. He fell silent and stared off into the middle distance.

"I believe him," he said finally. "No reason for the church to be beatin' up kids so they can build a school. One thing don't make sense, though."

"What's that?"

"Why Alvarez want to hold on to houses that are run-down and un-inhabited?"

"Maybe we should find out just how uninhabited those buildings really are. I hear looks can be deceiving."

8

I decided to go visit Street Business. It was in a big Victorian house on a quiet side street just beyond midtown Boston. The paint on the outside looked like a hippie's dream: a faded mustard, with purple trim on the turrets and other extremities.

There was a patch of lawn covered with dirty snow. The steps up to the front door, also painted purple, were icy.

There was no bell. I had called

Jackie that morning, and when I knocked he was at the door in seconds. "Hello, Spenser," he welcomed me, flashing his disconcerting teeth. "Come in, come in."

We entered a room where his thick hair gleamed in the ergonomic lighting. There were big overstuffed sofas and chairs scattered around a fifty-inch flat-screen television, and bookshelves filled with books along the walls. Boys' stuff was strewn around, jackets and a basketball, a PlayStation console and a batch of game cartridges. A baseball bat and a catcher's mitt. A couple of boys got to their feet. Well trained.

"Bobby and Sam, this is Mr. Spenser." The boys stuck out their hands, and we shook. Jackie said, "Boys, why don't you see about making yourselves some lunch."

Bobby and Sam went off. "The rest of them are working," Jackie said.

"How many live here?" I said.

"We've housed as many as twenty, but right now we have twelve. That includes a couple of Juan's guys, who help out. You know, they round up jobs, make sure the kids keep the place tidy." He took me into a small room where a man was working at a laptop. "Just talking about you," Jackie said. "Spenser, this is Pablo."

The man stood up. He was squat, with hair dyed the color of dark blue ink, wearing what looked like pale blue silk pajamas.

"Hello, Pablo," I said.

"Hi there." He gave me a smile that showed a lot of gold. "Jackie, I gotta talk to Juan. These books are a mess. You got to try to keep better records, kid."

"Can we do it later?" Jackie said. "I'm showing Spenser around right now."

Pablo sat back down and looked at what I recognized was a Quick-Books program.

Jackie led me through the house. There was one big central space upstairs with several beds set up dormitory-style and six other bedrooms, along with three decent-looking bathrooms. Downstairs was a kitchen, where some men were cooking tortillas. The air was rich with their smell.

Another room held a small gym with a couple of stationary bikes, an ancient treadmill, and a couple of punching bags.

"These get much use?" I motioned to the bags.

"Some," Jackie said. "I've been trying to get some guys around here to volunteer time to give the boys some pointers on boxing and wrestling, that sort of thing," Jackie said.

"For sport, or protection?"

"Both," Jackie said. "Some of the boys need to toughen up a bit. Others need their aggression channeled into something with rules and finesse."

"Ever hear of Harbor Health Club, Henry Cimoli's place? Henry's a friend. He can probably get you some equipment, if that would help. Headgear, gloves, mitts, mouth guards, that kind of thing."

"That would be terrific, Spenser." Jackie looked sincere and enthusiastic, but it was hard for me to tell. He had an open, boyish face, which gave away little. "I'm guessing you did some boxing. You any good?"

"Float like a butterfly, sting like a bee," I said. "Of course, the broken nose might tell you otherwise."

Jackie grinned. "I wasn't going to mention that." He made a half-hearted jab at a speed bag. "Any chance I could convince you to come by sometime and show the boys how it's done?"

"They probably already know how to get their noses broken," I said. If I was to find out who was trying to close down Jackie's business and why, spending some time on the premises might be a smart idea. And I liked Jackie's spirit. Upbeat. Relentlessly so. "But I'd be happy to teach them how not to."

"That would be great!" Jackie said.

We walked back into the front hall. The worn wooden floorboards creaked beneath our feet.

"No girls here?" I said.

"No," said Jackie. "We're trying to instill structure and discipline here. Boys reach a certain age, being around girls too much is counterproductive to the goal."

"Boys need to learn how to act around girls sometime."

"First things first, Spenser," Jackie said. "A young man must learn to respect himself before he can learn to respect others." His voice was solemn. I couldn't tell if he was parroting a self-help book or recounting a painful experience.

He walked me to the door. A scruffy, heavyset guy dressed in jeans and a sweatshirt stood just inside the open door, inhaling a cigarette. About thirty pounds of unnecessary stomach spilled over the jeans.

"This is Joe," Jackie said. He

sounded and looked as happy to see Joe as I did to hear "Rudolph the Red-Nosed Reindeer."

"Joe," I said.

Joe didn't speak. He exhaled enough smoke to double the carbon footprint of metropolitan Boston. Then he flicked his cigarette out the front door. It bounced off the steps and fell into the snow.

"You know I don't allow smoking in this house," Jackie said.

"Bite me," Joe said. *Wow, class act.* The kind of guy you want around impressionable young boys.

"You'd better leave, Joe. I don't want you around the kids. You're nothing but trouble," Jackie said.

"I ain't your trouble," Joe said. "I'm the one protecting you and your little kindergarten here. Might be better for you to thank me once in a while, instead of riding my ass." He slouched off and out the door.

Jackie sighed as he watched Joe shamble down the stairs and fish a package of cigarettes out of his pants pocket.

"Sorry, Spenser," Jackie said. "He's one of Juan's men. He sent him over here to protect us. Sometimes I wonder if he's worse than no one at all." He gave a short shake of his head, as if to erase Joe from his memory. Then he brightened. "Thanks for coming over to see the place," he said. "Any progress yet on finding out who wants us gone?"

"Too soon to have much," I said. "But I'll let you know when I do."

"Thanks, Spenser," he said. "I need to make Street Business work. I don't want to let the kids down. I don't want . . ." His voice trailed off.

I gave him a wave and negotiated down the icy steps to my car. When I looked back, Jackie was bending over the side of the steps, fishing Joe's cigarette butt out of a snowbank.

9

Once in a great while, Susan asked me to escort her to one of her charity events. The most important one of the year was to take place ten days before Christmas and would be held at the Taj. The cause was Meals with Heart, which provided free food to those in Boston who had fallen through other social-program nets.

We were on our way to the Taj on the appointed night.

"You look stunning," she said.

I was wearing a navy blue cash-
mere blazer she had given to me,
made probably by hand by clois-
tered nuns on a remote Scottish
isle. She had chosen a navy-and-
red striped silk necktie, which I was
told was Hermès but to my eye
could have been Syms. A crisp
white shirt, the neck a bit too snug
for my liking, and dark gray slacks
completed my ensemble. As a form
of silent protest, I wore black loaf-
ers polished to a high gloss with no
socks. Still, I felt like I was going
off to dancing school. Susan was
resplendent in a crimson satin
gown that showed off her perfect
skin. As she would be giving a
speech at the dinner, she had
sought the services of a profes-

sional makeup artist, though I thought it was gilding the lily. She sparkled.

"Brad and Angelina," I said.

"Too many kids."

"You've got a point." We made our way to the elevator.

Though all eyes would be on her, I knew Susan liked having me there. Knowing it was only for her was all that made it worthwhile.

We came into the huge ballroom hung with Christmas decorations, where we got the sticky labels with our names on them to put on and therefore ruin our outfits, and place cards with our table number. Ours was predictably table one, right up front by the dance floor. The Beantown Swing Orchestra was performing Glenn Miller's "Moonlight Serenade" as we found our seats.

"I detect a bar at the back of the room," I said. "Can I get you something?"

"God, no," Susan said. "Not until I'm done with my speech. I wouldn't want to embarrass myself." As self-possessed as she was in virtually all other situations, Susan was invariably nervous before giving speeches, and unfailingly flawless in her delivery.

"That would be an impossibility," I said. "But I need a strong beverage to steel myself for this crowd." I headed off toward the bar.

When I returned with my martini, others had joined our table. They stood, and we introduced ourselves.

Everyone's names matched their name tags. A tall, tanned Hispanic man in black tie bowed formally and said, "My name is Juan Alvarez. I'm happy to meet you, Mr. and Mrs. Spenser."

Susan put out her hand. "Dr. Susan Silverman. Nice to meet you, too."

"Spenser," I said. Direct.

"This is my friend Carmen," Alvarez said.

A tall, slender young woman with movie-star good looks smiled and shook Susan's hand, then mine. She wore a tight-fitting blue silk jacket, black slacks, and turquoise drop earrings. Her eyes were the color of lapis lazuli. Her handshake told me she was stronger than she looked.

"Of course, Dr. Silverman," Alvarez said. "My apologies. You are the force behind this whole endeavor. Congratulations on your fine work. We on the board are very proud of your achievements."

"Thank you, Mr. Alvarez," Susan said.

"Please — Juan," Alvarez said.

"Susan," Susan said with a radiant smile.

I took a long swallow of my drink and eyed Carmen over the rim of my glass. She looked back at me and smiled. She had very white teeth, full lips, and a tan in December.

A large middle-aged woman in a flowing floral gown approached the microphone and gave an elaborate throat-slashing signal to the band. Apparently, the program would precede dinner, which had both advantages and disadvantages. In my vast experience accompanying Susan to charity events, I learned that pre-dinner programs tended to be shorter, and permitted a quick departure once the table was cleared. On the other hand, listening to speeches on an empty stomach made me want to chew on the tablecloth, which Susan frowned upon. I settled in and covertly eyed the bread basket.

The large woman was wrapping it up. "And so I introduce our patron saint and great friend, Dr. Susan Silverman."

I had missed the preamble because I had been trying to catch the eye of a waiter for a refill of my drink. With success.

Susan made her usual brief and intelligent speech, which was met with thunderous applause, due to both its brevity and its excellence. Then the auction began. A portly, ruddy-faced man in black tie and tails took the stage and launched into the familiar rapid cadence of a professional auctioneer. His associates prowled among the tables, eagerly pointing out frantic bidders in case the auctioneer somehow missed the manic waving of bidding paddles. The crowd, fueled by alcohol, a competitive nature, and a compassionate spirit, shed its reserve and became boisterous. There were books autographed by local authors, Celtics tickets, and Cape Cod resort vacations, each lot more enticing than the last, all sold at prices far above any reasonable measure of value. Finally, the auctioneer announced the last lot, the most prized item of the evening.

"And now we are excited to present one of the greatest tennis players in the world, winner of the U.S. Open, two-time winner at Wimbledon, winner of the Australian Open, French Open, and too many other Grand Slam events to name. In short, a supreme athlete. Come on up here, Carmen, to announce the fabulous prize that awaits our top bidder!"

Our tablemate rose and went up to the stage. Now I remembered her. I was not a tennis fan, but I had caught one or two of her matches while surfing for Red Sox games in the past. She had disappeared from the tennis world a few years ago.

Next to the auctioneer, Carmen stood tall, her lean body in perfect proportion. Her voice was strong and low and resonant.

"I have two front-row box seats to next year's U.S. Open, including meals at a variety of four-star New York City restaurants, plus entertainment, travel, and lodging." She waved the tickets in the air, and the professional auctioneer started the bidding. Again, the crowd exploded. The bidding continued for several minutes, until only two competitors remained. They were both trim, well-dressed captains of industry, sitting at adjacent tables. Neither of them appeared accustomed to losing. They traded bids with authority, slowing the pace by raising the stakes in ever-smaller increments. They were cheered on by the admiring crowd and by what appeared to be matching trophy wives. Finally, the combatant at the table nearest us signaled surrender, and when further cajoling by the auctioneer failed to elicit another bid, the gavel went down. The winner paid $100,000 for the week and the thrill of victory. I wondered if he'd be as excited about the price of victory tomorrow morning.

Dinner was served with efficiency as soon as the auction ended. Our dinner companions were surprisingly pleasant and engaging. No one pontificated about politics. No one prattled on about their jewelry or wine collection. Everyone liked the Red Sox's chances come spring.

The event began to wind down after coffee. "I just have to thank a few people," Susan said, touching my hand, before walking off into the crowd. I was alone at the table with Juan Alvarez. Carmen was standing by the podium, surrounded by admirers.

"I've met your brother Jackie," I said.

Alvarez smiled. "Really? Dear

Joachim, the youngest of my siblings. How do you know him, if I may ask?"

"He came to me for help. He's under the impression someone is trying to drive him and his organization out of their home. I understand you own property on the same block."

Alvarez apparently found something interesting in the centerpiece and shifted his gaze in that direction. "I do own quite a lot of real estate in Boston." He smiled. "Isn't Carmen something?"

"Yes. She still play?"

"Not professionally. She had to retire. Bad knees, you know. It happens to . . ." He stopped as Carmen approached and sat down.

"You did very well," he said to her.

"Thank you, Juan. It's a good cause. Dr. Silverman does good work."

"That she does." I smiled dashingly. Something about her reminded me of Ava Gardner.

"Have you two met before?" Alvarez said. His smile belied the vague accusatory undercurrent in his tone.

"Never," I said.

"We Puerto Ricans say that we met in another life," she said. "But Juan, I met you in this life and that is all you need to know." She leaned over and kissed him on his cheek.

She looked up at me. I was standing, ready to go. "Good to meet you, Spenser."

"Yes, Spenser, I hope you and Susan will come out to see us at the farm in Weston. I'll arrange it," Alvarez said, and stood up to shake my hand. He had a thin scar that ran from his left eye to his mouth. I hadn't noticed it before. His eyes were round and very dark, and despite his incessant smile, I saw an expression of what I imagined a hawk would look like at the instant it swooped down on the rabbit in the meadow.

"That would be delightful," I said, and saw Susan coming across the room to save me.

10

The next day Hawk and I drove to Weston, where both the old and new rich had big horse farms and eighteenth-century houses or Mc-Mansions and at least twenty acres of land each to keep them on, all just fifteen minutes from downtown Boston. We were sitting in my car, off the road but within view of the Alvarez compound. Snow sifted down and veiled the pastures before us. We had coffee and donuts. The heater was on, and it was still cold inside.

I had done a little research on Alvarez. A Google search and a short conversation with Susan, but it still qualified as research. Google told me that Juan Alvarez graduated from the London School of Economics. Worked in London for a few years at Morgan Stanley. There was an early marriage to a British woman and a divorce five years later. No children. Then the bio stopped and picked up again in Boston. His import/export firm's success was noted, and his philanthropic interests included everything from large donations to the Boston Symphony to Dana-Farber research to Meals with Heart.

"Why do you suppose Juan Alvarez lives at the hotel Taj instead of getting himself a swell condo at One Charles or someplace more befitting his image?" I said.

"Somehow a hotel more loose," said Hawk. "You come, you go. No one notices or cares. Plus he got this fine farm."

"Good point," I said. "Why have a place in Boston at all?"

Hawk yawned. "Pied-à-terre, babe," he said. "All rich white boys got a pied-à-terre in the big city. Place to do the things you don't want no one to know about back on the farm."

"And somehow he became Father Flanagan and Santa Claus and a prince of Boston high society all rolled into one. In most big cities, all you need is money to give to the key charities. They have to put you on the board. Before you know it, as long as you don't eat your peas with a knife, you're invited to all the best parties," I said.

"I prefer my peas on a knife," Hawk said.

"They tend to frown on switchblades at fancy dinner parties," I said. "You'd probably feel out of place."

"Not the only reason I'd feel out of place," Hawk said. He looked out toward the Alvarez house. "We have a plan here? Or we just gonna sit here till we run out of gas."

"No plan," I said. "But we do have choices. One, we sit and watch, or two, move and stir things up. Right now we're sitting and watching."

"How 'bout I take a nap till we get to the move-and-stir-things-up part of the program?"

"Suit yourself," I said. "But don't expect me to share all the important clues with you if I find them while you're asleep."

"Already know what you gonna learn. Gonna learn when the mail gets delivered. Gonna learn how long it take that icicle on the roof gutter to melt. Ain't gonna learn nothin' we need to know, like what goes on over there and how many guns they got on the place. They could be building weapons of mass destruction in the side yard and we ain't gonna learn that, sittin' where we are."

I sipped my coffee and looked at the big colonial house. There was a Jeep parked off to the side of a long circular driveway. I could see the Christmas wreath on the front door. I could see the icicle hanging from the roof gutter. I couldn't see any signs of life or activity. Knowing when the mail got delivered wasn't going to help me. And that icicle wasn't going to melt for a long time.

"Okay, you win," I said. "Saddle up, Kemosabe. Let's go look at some horses."

I drove slowly down the road that led to the smaller houses on the property, where I supposed employees lived. At the end of the road I could see a large barn and what looked like a long, low stable. There were fences with those three black slats you see in photos of Kentucky horse farms. Maybe all horse fences had them. An emblem.

It was early afternoon and no one was at home.

The snow was thick now, and blurred my vision. I squinted.

In front of us in the middle of the dirt road, looking like a snow bunny, was a short, squat man holding a rifle. It was pointed at my head. I stopped the car, pulled the Beretta from my shoulder holster, and dropped my gun hand to my side. I knew Hawk would be doing the same.

The man held his rifle on me and

approached my side of the car. I rolled down the window.

"Excuse me," I said. "Is this the way to Pottery Barn?"

It took a bit longer than I would have expected for him to comprehend what I was saying. I could see him almost mouthing the words until they sunk in.

"There's no fucking Pottery Barn out here, asshole. This here is private property, and you're trespassing."

"That's what I thought," I said, "but try telling that to Clarabelle."

The man leaned in to look into the car and squinted at Hawk. Hawk slowly turned his head toward the man and flashed an even smile.

"Who the hell is Clarabelle?" the man said.

"The navigation system in my car," I said. "I like to give a name to the voice that gives the directions. Makes it more personal, don't you think?"

Rifle Man was mouthing the words again. I waited.

"Listen, smart-ass. This here is private property, and you're trespassing." He repeated the lines, as if he had been trained to say them, which was probably the case. Those words, backed up by the gun, were probably enough to scare off most interlopers.

"Okay," I said. "So it's not a Pottery Barn. What goes on out here? Bird sanctuary?"

He brought the gun back up level with my head. I pulled the Beretta up to my lap.

Someone came out of the cottage to my left. A short, dark woman with a child. She spoke in Spanish to the man with the rifle. I understood enough to know her child was sick and that she needed a ride to the emergency room.

Rifle Man became flustered and annoyed. He tried to keep his gun trained on me while he barked back at the woman. Clearly, multitasking wasn't his strength. I couldn't understand all that he was saying, but his tone didn't convey sympathy. The woman started to cry, and there was desperation in her voice that required no translation.

"You understand this?" I said to Hawk.

"Woman's baby be really sick. She say he need to get to the hospital right away. He say that too bad, he ain't bringing them to the hospital, don't care if the baby live or not."

The woman rushed closer to the man, pleading and wailing and trying to show him her sick child. He pushed her away, and she and the baby fell to the ground.

Hawk opened his door and got out of the car.

"Hey! Hey!" Rifle Man swung his rifle over the top of the car toward Hawk. "Stop right there or I'll shoot. This here's private property and you're trespassing."

Hawk ignored him and walked around the car to the woman and her baby. As Rifle Man swiveled to train his gun on Hawk, I pushed open my car door and slammed it into his left side. He collapsed with a grunt and the rifle flew from his hands, landing a few feet away. I stepped from the car. As Rifle Man tried to stand, I leaned in and kicked him in the stomach. He fell to the ground and rolled onto his back. I stood over him with my Beretta pointed at his nose.

"Okay," I said. "Here's the deal. We're taking this young woman and her baby to the hospital. You're going to pull yourself together, and in two hours you are going to drive to the hospital and pick them up.

Do you understand me?"

Rifle Man was having an even harder time with comprehension. I waited for him to mouth the words and then digest them. Finally, he nodded.

"You have dented my car door, and worse than that, you've annoyed us. Being men of goodwill in this holiday season, we're willing to forgive you. But if you try to stop us, or if you cause any harm to this woman or her child, I am going to come back here and extract my insurance deductible from you. Do you understand that?"

Again he mouthed the words. He seemed to have problems with "extract." I tried again.

"If you shoot at us, or if you harm

the woman or her baby, I will come back here and hurt you. Do you understand?"

Fear materialized on Rifle Man's face, and this time he nodded without having to do much thinking. He shouted something in rapid-fire Spanish to the woman.

"Hawk?" I said.

"He tell our new friend here that he'll come by the hospital in two hours to check on her and the bambino. He also tell her he hope the baby be okay."

I holstered my Beretta, walked over to the rifle, cracked open the barrel and collected the shells and put them in my pocket. Then I grabbed the rifle by the barrel with both hands and flung it over the car and far into the trees.

Hawk had led the woman and the baby over to my car and put them in the backseat. I got back in the car, did a three-point turn, and drove slowly back out the dirt road. In my rearview mirror, I could see Rifle Man slowly getting to his knees and looking dumbly at our taillights.

We reached the open highway, and she said, *"A la derecha."* I could see in the rearview mirror that she was young, maybe twenty. She wore her hair in a kind of bun, and her winter coat was patched and threadbare. The baby wore a good-quality parka and was nestled down in it, asleep.

Hawk said, *"Cómo se llama?"*

"Martita. *Mi hijo se llama* Juanito. *Tiene mucho fiebre.*"

"*Habla inglés?*" Hawk said.

"*Sí. Un poco.*" She smiled and I could see she was missing a front tooth and the rest of them looked brown.

"Do you know Carmen?" I said.

"*Sí, sí! Es un angel!*" She smiled some more. "She is my amiga."

"Your friend. And Slide?" I said.

"*Sí.* She takes care of him." She smiled and shook her head slowly. "He is like a little brother to her."

"Do they live near you?" I said.

"*Sí, sí.*" She put her hands together.

"Carmen lives with you, not at the big house?" I said.

"*Sí, sí.*" She smiled some more.

"Por uno o dos días.

"Ah! *A la izquierda!"* she added.

"Left," Hawk said.

Halfway down the block in a storefront was a medical building. A line of people, looking miserable in the cold, waited to get inside. Above them, the Christmas decorations, big red bells and candy canes and sleighs with Santa in them, were hung along the lines between the telephone poles. Hawk got out with Martita. She was headed to go to the end of the line, but Hawk took her under the arm and marched her into the building. I thought I would let him take care of this situation. He could be very convincing when he wanted to be. I watched the line of people —

men, women, and children, all sick with something — patiently waiting to get medical attention, at a place that looked nothing like Mass General.

Hawk returned, quicker than I would have thought.

"I told them I was President Obama's cousin," he said.

"See how well the health-care system works," I said, "when you give it a chance."

11

I had promised Jackie I'd drop by
Street Business to give his charges
a boxing lesson. We agreed on a
time that fit my hectic holiday
schedule, and I had imposed upon
Henry Cimoli to scrounge up some
used equipment for me to bring.
Because Hawk was curious about
Street Business, I invited him
along. I also invited him because I
couldn't carry all the equipment by
myself.

On the way to the house on Curtis Street, Hawk said, "You going to a lot of trouble for this Jackie fellow. Christmas spirit?"

"Maybe. I remember my father and uncles teaching me how to box when I was about ten. Learned a lot. Not just how to move my feet."

Hawk was silent. After a moment or two he said, "You know Jackie's kids, they different from you. Come from a different place."

I glanced at Hawk. He was looking at the road ahead, expressionless. "Worth a try," I said.

Jackie had cleared the exercise room and put down some canvas on the floor, flat and neat and secure. When Hawk and I arrived, he and four of the boys were waiting for me. They all wore sweats and high-top sneakers.

I introduced Hawk and Jackie. Jackie offered us both coffee, which we declined.

"How goes Street Business?" I said. "Everything quiet?"

"Since I came to see you," Jackie said.

"The Christmas lull."

Jackie turned to the boys. "This is Mr. Spenser," he said, "and his friend Hawk. They've offered to show you boys some basics of boxing. Please introduce yourselves and welcome our new friend."

The tallest boy, but not necessarily the oldest, stepped forward. "I'm Teddy," he said. He had red hair, freckles, and pale blue eyes, and was thin as paint. We shook hands.

Next was Mike. A pudgy kid with a wide grin. "We heard about you, Mr. Spenser. Jackie says you're a tough guy," he said.

"Ram tough," I said, "but I use my power only for good."

There was Pedro, one of Juan's immigrant kids, who had a baby face and looked about ten, and Carl, who was the oldest and had started to shave. He sported a small scraggly beard and lank blond hair.

Carl's expression conveyed either disdain or a severe stomach cramp. "I know how to box already," he said.

"Good," Jackie said. "Then you don't have to stay. No need to waste our guests' time." His rebuke was friendly but firm. Carl stayed.

Hawk and I unloaded the used mitts, gloves, and headgear from Henry, as well as the mouth guards from a local sporting goods store. Jackie passed out the equipment while I surveyed the room. There were two bags attached to opposite walls, one a heavy bag and the other a speed bag. Some jump ropes. Some hand wraps strung over the back of a bench.

"Okay," I said. "Any of you do any running? Or any other exercise?" I said.

"Naw," Mike said. They all shook their heads. "We ride our bikes, that count?" Teddy said.

"Sure. But boxing takes both strength and endurance, maybe

more than any other sport. You have to be in good shape," I said. "So the first thing we're going to do today is run in place and jump some rope."

Carl sneered. "Jump rope's for girls," he said.

Hawk looked at him. "Jump rope's for athletes," he said.

I handed out the ropes. One to Teddy, one to Pedro, and one to Hawk the athlete. "Mike, you run in place with me," I said. "We'll try five minutes. Come on, Jackie, you up for this?" He grinned at the challenge and grabbed a jump rope.

Five minutes later the three boys were red-faced and puffing. "You guys ain't even breathing hard," Mike said. "Neither's Jackie."

"We've had a lot of practice," I said. "If you want to box, you need to do this every day. And look, the fun part."

Hawk and I took the hand wraps and put them on the boys' hands in figure eights, fitting them snugly on their small hands. Then we put mitts on them and took them over to the speed bag. "Try hitting it, any way you want, just to get the feel of it," I said. "Take turns."

"You box?" I said to Jackie.

"A little," he said. "But I can mix it up with them anytime. Today's for the professionals to show their stuff."

The kids had stepped up to the speed bag one by one, and flailed away, missing it most of the time, laughing and jabbing one another in the ribs, and dancing around the bag. Carl watched. He had put on wraps. He went over, picked up a pair of old leather boxing gloves, and went to the heavy bag. He stepped up to it and whacked it like an amateur, but with some strength. I held the bag for him. He went at it again.

"Good," I said. "Next we'll work on your footwork."

"Don't need to," Carl said. He was starting to breathe heavily. "Footwork's fine."

I pushed the heavy bag slightly, and Carl's next punch hit the side and brushed off. His momentum carried him forward, and he tripped. He staggered through the punch and stumbled to the floor.

The others kids stopped and stared at him. Pedro and Mike stifled laughs in their gloves.

"Hey!" Carl said. "That's not fair. You tricked me."

"You don't have to worry about footwork if you're hitting something that's stationary," I said. "Problem with people is they tend to move. If you're going to box something that has feet, you've got to have good footwork."

I put my hand down to help him up. He pushed my hand away and pulled himself to his feet.

"Okay," I said. "Let's try it again. This time I promise I won't move the bag. We'll work on footwork next time."

Carl ripped into the bag with a sullen fury. After a few punches his pace slowed, and in less than a minute he was spent.

Hawk and I worked with the other three kids for the next half-hour. When they finished, the boys piled the equipment back into the boxes.

Pedro said, "Will you return and teach us some more?"

We nodded.

"In the meantime," I said, "take good care of that equipment. It's yours now."

The boys and Jackie beamed. "Say thank you to Mr. Spenser and Hawk, boys. That's very generous of them."

The boys responded with a uniform singsong chorus of thanks.

Even Carl managed a grudging "Thanks, man."

Jackie smiled, then turned to the boys. "When you are boxing, boys, your hands are your weapons. You need to know how to use them, and when. Mastering any weapon is about discipline and control. That's it for today. You guys go get something to eat," Jackie said.

The boys bolted in the direction of the kitchen. Carl's elbows put him in the lead.

"Sorry about Carl," Jackie said. "He's a hard nut to crack. Been here about six months. He served time as a juvenile for breaking and entering, vandalism, car theft. You know. Pretty much kid stuff."

"Just enough to get thrown in

with guys tougher than him," Hawk said.

Jackie looked at Hawk and nodded. "You got it. All these kids got a story. The Mexicans came over the border in Arizona being shot at; some of them saw a mother or father killed in front of them and somehow got away and reached relatives and made their way east. You take a kid like Teddy?"

"The tall one," I said.

"Yeah. Good kid. But both parents were drunks and they dumped him. Just left him at an orphanage in Philadelphia. He had been there most of his life until he ran away and we found him. Or he found us is more like it. There's a network of these lost street kids from city to city, and they hear about safe places to go. Some want to get there, some have already given up. These kids are so beaten up by living by the time we get them, I spend a lot of time just getting them to trust me."

"What give you the idea to start Street Business?" Hawk said.

Jackie looked at Hawk. "I've always wanted to be like my big brother, Juan. A big success. Great with women. Lots of money. But it didn't turn out that way for me. I tried a lot of things. Gambling. Selling cars. I wasn't good at any of them. But I always liked kids. And I was lucky. My parents were good to us. As you know, my mother still lives in Lawrence, and my sisters and brothers all live nearby. Except, of course, Juan."

"Yes, of course, Juan," I said.

"You don't like my brother?" Jackie looked surprised.

"I don't know him well enough to like him or not like him. I've only met him once. He does seem like an international man of mystery."

"He's always been good to me, Spenser. And to our family. He has been generous with the fruits of his success. Without him, these kids would just be more sad stories out there on the streets. Because of Juan, they at least have a chance."

"And because of you," I said. "Probably more than Juan."

Jackie shrugged as he stood. "I got to get a shower and do some chores. Thanks for coming by to-day. Both of you. The kids loved their boxing lesson."

A stocky guy about my size was leaning on the wall just inside the front door, filling the space oc-cupied by Joe on my last visit. He was wearing gray sweatpants over running shoes, and a New England Patriots sweatshirt with a matching slouch cap. He straightened up as Hawk and I approached.

"You security?" I said.

His lipped curled to form some-thing that could have been a grin or a sneer.

"Security. Bus driver. Truant offi-cer. Handyman," he said. "Any-thing they need around this hell-hole."

"Let me guess," I said. "You didn't volunteer for this duty."

"Christ, no." The guy gave a short snort. "Volunteer." He spat out the word like it described an unnatural act. "I'm minding my own business out in the suburbs, the boss says, 'Frankie, get your ass into Boston and keep my little brother from falling into the Charles.' The boss speaks, I jump. So here I am."

"The boss would be Juan Alvarez?"

Frankie stiffened and pulled himself away from the wall.

"Who wants to know?"

"My name's Spenser. This is Hawk. Jackie asked me to help find out who's been causing problems for Street Business."

Frankie relaxed and resumed his job holding up the wall.

"Lucky you. Heard about you. Super-dick come to save the day. Good luck."

I let that pass. "What can you tell me about what's been going on around here?"

Frankie rolled his eyes and exhaled elaborately. "Nothing going on around here. A few kids get their lunch money stolen on their way home from work." He rallied himself from the wall to put air quotations around "work," then settled back again. "Some get in fights and get knocked around a little. Chickenshit stuff."

"Still," I said. "Hard to believe, with all the crack security around here."

He straightened up again and leaned into my face. "Screw you, Jack," he said. "It all happens out on the street somewhere. Never had a problem in the yard or in the premises."

"It's Spenser," I said. "And I think you mean 'on the premises.' Any idea who might be harassing the kids?"

Frankie folded his arms across his chest. I had a feeling we were experiencing his entire repertoire of poses.

"Don't know, don't care. Kids go out on the city streets and some get into fights. That's a big fucking news flash. Especially with these turds. This ain't exactly a collection of altar boys."

"I'm sensing you're not a big fan of Street Business."

"You think? Best thing anyone could do is run these pissants off and take a wrecking ball to the place. Or maybe lock them in here and bring in the wrecking ball."

"So you're not a believer in Jackie's mission to help kids?"

Frankie shook his head. "Guy's got his head up his ass. He thinks if he clothes and feeds street kids they'll grow up and save the world. Christ, these kids are animals. You dress 'em up and give 'em three squares a day, they're still animals. Just as likely to kill Jackie in his bed as anything."

"So you just give up and let them

be animals?"

"You let their families take care of them. That's the way I was brought up."

"And if they don't have family?" Hawk asked. Until then he had been silent, and his question startled Frankie.

Frankie recovered. "That's bullshit. Everyone's got family. If the parents aren't around, there are aunts and uncles and grandparents. And if there aren't any relatives, send 'em back where they came from."

"Your boss aware of your enlightened views of his brother and his work?" I said.

"You ask him straight, I bet he'd agree with me. Juan Alvarez is one tough sonovabitch. He started with nothing and clawed his way to the top. No one gave him any handouts. He had his family and himself, and that's it. And family is everything to Mr. Alvarez. He looks out for his own. I seen the way he supports his mother and his brothers and sisters. Especially Jackie."

"Especially Jackie?"

"Yeah." Frankie shook his head. "From what I hear, Jackie's the black sheep. Always getting into trouble. Mr. Alvarez promised his mother that he'd take Jackie under his wing, straighten him out. When Jackie decides he wants to start this Romper Room, Mr. Alvarez sets him up and supports him, just like he promised Mama."

"Doesn't Alvarez support a bunch of charities around Boston? Street Business seems to fit with that."

Frankie unfolded his arms and put them behind his back. Experimenting with a new pose. Conversational Frankie. Daring.

"Mr. Alvarez donates to groups that have been around a long time, that have a track record. Places that do things you can point to. Stuff connected to his businesses. Lot better places to put money than this rat hole."

"You ever consider following the kids around, try to find out who's bothering them?"

"Yeah, right." Frankie flashed the might-be-a-sneer, might-be-a-grin look at Hawk. Hawk showed nothing. The look disappeared. "I do what Mr. Alvarez tells me to do. No upside in freelancing."

"Might help you to move around a little bit," I said. "You stand next to the door too long, people might mistake you for a coatrack."

Frankie balled his fists, took a step toward me, then looked at Hawk and reconsidered. We walked out.

12

Hawk and I sat in my car and looked back at Street Business. We seemed to be doing a lot of sitting in my car lately. Maybe it was the start of a new holiday tradition. Next year we could change it up a little and sit in Hawk's car.

"How you feeling about Street Business now?" I said.

Hawk nodded his approval. "Not bad," he said. "This Jackie seem sincere, seem good with the kids. Place be clean and tidy. Kids look happy, like they gettin' fed and looked after. Got structure and routine."

"Is it a place you would have wanted to be when you were a kid?"

Hawk shook his head.

"Not what I wanted, way I was then. Didn't want no structure, didn't want no rules."

"But you wanted to eat. A place to sleep."

"Food always come with some catch. Rules. Trade-offs. Someone tryin' to save me. Didn't want that. Needed to find my own way."

"So — what, then?"

"Man I am now can look back, say sure, would'a been nice to have someplace safe to go, place where you knew somebody give a rat's ass, could teach you things. Didn't want that then."

He turned to me and grinned. " 'Course, I lived in a place like that, probably grow up to be a minister. Or worse, an Afro-American you."

"We so different?"

"Different enough. You got rules."

"And you don't?"

"Just a few. Need a whole book for your rules. Have to think too much. Turns you soft sometimes. I try to live your way, I be dead long ago."

"And you think Street Business might make those kids soft?"

"Just sayin' the world be a pretty simple place when you just tryin' to stay alive." He fell silent for a moment. "Street Business be good if it gives kids a safe place off the streets. Even better if it teach them skills. Someday they got to go out on their own, leave Street Business behind. Got to be ready when that day comes."

"Give a man a fish versus teach a man to fish."

"Always comforting to hear you quote Scripture," Hawk said.

"Anything trouble you about this place?"

Hawk thought for a moment. "Couple of things. Something go wrong down here, sure would hate to depend on ol' Frankie."

"Yeah," I said. "You've got to admire a man who loves his work. I've met the other member of the security detail. He's pretty much the same."

"Don't know this Juan Alvarez, but you think if he so concerned about his brother, he make sure his team fell in line."

"Or bring in a team that did," I said. "What else?"

Hawk looked out the car window. "Neighborhood's too quiet."

He was right. The block was deserted. Except for Street Business, there were no lights visible in the windows of any building on either side of the street. There were no Christmas lights, no menorahs, no holiday decorations for the length of the block. I realized that in the entire time Hawk and I had been in the car, we had seen no traffic, no pedestrians, no kids pulling sleds or throwing snowballs.

We waited and watched for signs of life. Fifteen minutes passed and nothing changed.

"No Whos in Whoville," I said.

"Maybe the Rapture just happened," said Hawk, "and we got left behind."

Dusk settled over the neighborhood. The streetlights kicked on, offering a thin canopy of light over the street.

"Still curious why Alvarez don't wanna sell these houses," Hawk said.

"Well," I said, opening my car door, "since we're in the neighborhood, let's find out what makes them so special."

The first one we chose was quiet and dark inside. If anyone was upstairs, we did not hear them. I turned on a couple of lamps in a room that once had passed as a parlor but now looked like the final resting place for furniture the Salvation Army wouldn't take. The two sofas were sprung, and the chair cushions looked as greasy as two-day-old stir-fry.

In the kitchen, dirty dishes were piled in the sink and laundry was heaped by the washer.

"Tidy bunch," Hawk said.

"No sports equipment or video games. Nothing for kids."

"These aren't kids. These employees," Hawk said.

I entered a larger room with a

desk in the corner. I was shuffling through some papers lying on the scarred Formica top when I heard footsteps.

I turned, and a tall man with a red crew cut was pointing a small handgun at me. Hawk was nowhere in sight.

"Who are you?" he said. "What are you doing here?" He was lean and strong-looking, in better shape than either Joe or Frankie at Street Business.

"I'm going door-to-door collecting for charity," I said. "We want to send all the underprivileged kids in Weston to violin camp. Would you care to contribute?"

"Not funny, asshole," Redhead said. "Hands up where I can see them."

I raised my hands, and he continued to point the gun at my chest. He seemed uncertain about what to do next.

"How'd you get in here?" Redhead was doing his best to look menacing. The gun helped.

"Chimney," I said. "Just like Santa."

Redhead opened his mouth to say something. He never got the chance. Hawk appeared behind him and put one arm around Redhead's neck and his knee deep into his back. Redhead let out a choked snarl and dropped his gun. I picked it up and stuck it in my pocket.

Hawk let Redhead go.

I looked down at the floor where

Redhead sat with his head down. He had left a small duffel bag in the doorway, which I inspected while Hawk watched him. Five hundred in big bills and a round-trip economy ticket to El Paso, Texas. A small notepad filled with dates and numbers. I tucked it inside my pocket.

I looked at Redhead. "You live here?"

He stared at the ground and said nothing.

"Want to tell us what's so great about El Paso at Christmas?"

Redhead remained enamored with a spot on the wooden floor. He shook his head.

"Maybe he just shy," said Hawk. "Could use a little encouragement to facilitate some conversation."

Redhead started to shake a little.

"No," I said. "Let's go."

"No?" Hawk said. "Guy almost shot you."

"Almost," I said. "And we did invite ourselves in."

Hawk shook his head. "Rules, Spenser. Rules gonna get you killed someday."

"Maybe," I said. "But not today."

13

I was sitting at my desk with my feet up, contemplating the cooking of the turducken for our Christmas dinner. It needed to roast for seven hours. I was counting backward from our appointed dinner hour of two in the afternoon to figure out when it should go in Susan's oven. Then the door to my office opened and Juan Alvarez came in.

"I hope you don't mind the intrusion," he said. His tone suggested he didn't much care whether I minded or not. He carried his overcoat on his arm. He wore a tweed jacket with smooth leather patches at the elbows, a tartan vest, and a green tie patterned with small yellow animals that looked like little foxes.

I motioned to the chair opposite my desk.

He shot me a baleful look with his hard brown eyes. "You, Spenser, are not who you say you are. You are a private investigator. You never mentioned that when we were introduced." He sounded genuinely injured.

"I also didn't tell you that I enjoy piña coladas and walks in the rain," I said. "And, I might add, you never asked."

"I hear that you or someone working with you has been snooping into my private affairs. If that's true, I'd like it to stop. I'm sure there must be some misunderstanding." He gave me a faint smile.

"What exactly have you heard, Juan?" I said.

"My foreman told me that you came out to my farm in Weston a few days ago. And one of my men in the city reports that you visited one of my properties recently. Each time with some black man. Each time one of my employees was attacked." He leaned forward toward me. "True?"

"A lot of people say that about Hawk," I said. "They look at him and say, 'That is some black man.' "

He got up. "This is not a joke to me, Spenser. You are interfering with how I run my business. I don't know what you're trying to do. I thought when we met the other night we met as friends. I still hope so." He paused. "But please understand. If you don't stop, I will stop you."

I let his words hang in the air for a moment.

"I'm sure you're serious, Juan," I said. "I'm also sure you are aware that someone has been threatening your brother and his boys' shelter. In fact, if you recall our delightful encounter at the charity auction, you might remember my informing you that Jackie had requested my help in making the threats stop."

"I am quite capable of protecting my brother," Alvarez said. "And I fail to see the connection between Jackie's problems and your invasion of my properties."

"Fair enough," I said. "My investigative methods may seem as opaque to you as your business dealings do to me. We both have an interest in knowing who might be threatening Jackie and Street Business. Any ideas?"

Alvarez's demeanor softened, and he sighed. "Jackie," he said. "He's tried so hard, and always manages to fail. His intentions are good, but that's not enough. Street Business is just a pipe dream, I'm afraid."

"It may be ambitious," I said.

"But who would want to see it fail?"

Alvarez shrugged. "Who knows? Anybody. Everybody. Maybe a gang that sees Street Business as an invasion of its turf. Drug dealers or other criminals who see it as a threat. So-called concerned citizens. Not everyone supports housing homeless kids in the community, as you might imagine. Even real estate developers, perhaps. We have had many offers to purchase our buildings on Curtis Street, mine as well as Jackie's."

"I'm curious, Juan," I said. "Why do you own so many properties on Curtis Street?"

He smiled without warmth. "I have many employees. There is not enough room for them all at my farm in Weston. And, frankly, I keep a couple of men in town to keep an eye on Jackie and Street Business, to make sure everything goes well."

"So why do you continue to support Street Business if you think it's a pipe dream?"

"Jackie is my brother, Spenser," he said. "He is family. I promised my mother that I would support and protect the family, Jackie most of all. As long as he believes in Street Business, I must not fail him. To do so would be to dishonor my mother and the memory of my father. That I won't do."

Alvarez gathered his coat and pulled a pair of leather gloves from his pocket.

"Thank you for your time, Spenser. I trust we have simply had a misunderstanding. I will take care of my brother. It is difficult with my travel schedule and business obligations, but he is my responsibility."

"I understand you travel quite a bit," I said. "I hope you get a break for the holidays. Any chance you're heading south of the border for New Year's?"

He put his gloved hand out to shake mine. "Merry Christmas, Spenser. May the New Year bring you peace and prosperity." His grip was strong and his smile cold.

14

The visit from Juan Alvarez had annoyed me enough that I abandoned my further thoughts of the turducken and decided to catch up with the sports section of *The Boston Globe* instead. Outside it looked cold, but the sun was shining. A few shoppers, bundled against the weather, clutched shopping bags as they hurried down the street. Patches of snow lay in irregular patterns across the Boston Garden.

My office door opened, and Carmen came in. She held out her hand. "Hello again, Spenser."

"Hello, Carmen."

Her hand was cold from the outdoors, and it looked like she bit her fingernails. She had a strong grip. She wore no makeup on her smooth, dark skin except for a touch of lipstick. She smiled at me. I smiled back. I wondered how it must feel to be a woman whose looks were so startling. The combination of her blue eyes and strong features was oddly electric. I sat down again behind my desk. And waited for her to begin.

She was wearing clean, well-worn blue jeans, work boots, and a blue-and-green checked wool shirt over a white tank top. She put her sheepskin parka on the back of my visitor's chair. Her hair was straight and fell to her shoulders, and was so dark it was almost black. She gave me an open, friendly look. And there were those eyes again.

"And what can I do for you?" I said.

"I hear you help people. Jackie told Slide, and Slide told me."

"Word gets around."

"Yes." She paused. "You know Jackie is Juan's younger brother?"

"Yes," I said. "Is that a problem?"

Carmen frowned. "Juan Alvarez is the reason I need your help."

"Maybe this would be easier if I offered you a cup of coffee?"

"Do you have anything stronger?" she said.

156

"My coffee is pretty strong," I said, "but yes, as a matter of fact, I do."

I pulled my emergency bottle of Johnnie Walker Blue and two water glasses from the cabinet against the wall, and grabbed the tray of ice cubes from the small refrigerator next to my desk. I dropped the ice cubes one at a time into the glasses and poured two fingers of scotch into each glass. I handed her one and returned to my desk with the other.

"How can I help?" I said.

Carmen took a sip of the scotch, rolled it around her mouth, then closed her eyes and swallowed. It was good to encounter a woman who enjoyed scotch.

"I come from a very poor area near San Juan. My father is Puerto Rican, my mother was Irish. She died when I was two. My dad had a lot of different jobs when I was growing up. Sometimes he drove a cab. Sometimes he gambled or dealt drugs. Small-time stuff. It was a shame, too, because he had a knack for sports. He played a little tennis and fell in love with the game. He put a racquet in my hand as soon as I could hold a doll. He saw what I could do, saw it could get us out of that slum we lived in." She looked at me hard.

I waited. She sipped her drink.

"Go on," I said.

"I was his ticket. I was a quick study, and he saw a way out. He coached me, just like a lot of parents have coached their kids in tennis. Parents coached both Martinas, Steffi Graf, the Williams sisters, all of us. My dad worked me very hard, but I loved it. And I was talented. I was headed for the big time. Started when I was eight and never looked back." Her voice rose slightly. "By the time I was twenty, I was playing Wimbledon, the Open. And not just playing. Winning."

I waited while she went back. I waited some more. Then I said, "What happened?"

She took a deep breath and focused on me again.

"The papers said that my knees went bad. I was only twenty-two, and I had to retire from professional tennis. The real story is a little different."

"You want to tell me about it?"

"I fought with my dad. I was rebellious and wanted to be independent. I thought I knew everything. He stopped coaching me and left the circuit in disgust. I went crazy from the fame and money. I was wild and tried everything that came my way. Booze, drugs, men, women, you name it. I was young and healthy and strong and did my workouts and continued my training no matter what else I did at night. And I was able to get away with it for a while." She took a swallow of her scotch and looked hard at me with her amazing eyes.

"You know how easy it is to throw everything away when you never had anything to begin with?"

I nodded.

"I thought I was invincible." She gave a mirthless laugh. "When I hit bottom, I hit pretty hard. I don't seem to do things halfway."

"And now?"

"A couple of years ago I got straightened out. There was a very rich man I had met in London when I was playing Wimbledon who now lives in Boston. I ran into him." She paused. "When we first met, I had no idea he knew my father, that his family had left the same bad neighborhood in Puerto Rico and come over here to live in Lawrence."

I nodded. "Juan Alvarez."

"Yes. Almost four years ago he got me into a rehab place, and after I got out he took me to live with him in Weston at his farm. He wants to get married, but that's not for me." She smiled. "I don't mind playing his hostess at his social events, and up until recently he's been good to me. I got bored sitting around while he traveled, which is a lot, so in my spare time I started giving tennis lessons to the area children, and some of the adults, too. People here have plenty of money for that. Juan loves tennis himself and built a beautiful all-weather tennis court in his big barn. Despite my ups and downs, I've kept in touch with my good friends, and once in a while I get a big-name player to come out for a match. So I've managed to rehab my reputation a bit as well."

"That's good to hear. But we haven't gotten to the why-you-need-me part," I said.

"Juan Alvarez is not the man I thought he was. When I knew him before, he was kind and gentle. And that is the way most people see him. But gradually I have learned that he can be vicious and cruel. He hides this side brilliantly, but now I see it. Until now, I managed to escape his temper, but when a runaway boy came to the barn out of nowhere and I befriended him, Juan was furious and ordered me to get rid of him or he would make him disappear. He was jealous of my affection for a lost boy, and I knew he meant he would do the boy great harm."

"Has he actually acted on his threats?"

"I have heard from some of his employees that he has had people beaten and tortured. Even killed. Sometimes for minor mistakes, silly things. Last week, a maid forgot to lock the front door of the house. Juan had one of his men slam the door on the woman's hand. He broke several bones in her hand."

"This may be a dumb question, but did she report it to the police?"

Carmen smiled without humor. "No," she said. "She is undocumented. Most of Juan's workers are. If they go to the police, they will be deported. He has also convinced them that worse things will happen."

"Like what?"

"Many of the workers have children. If the parents try to leave or make trouble, they fear Juan will harm their children, or they will never see their children again. He encourages that fear."

"Because they are illegal, they have no protection from him."

"Yes. I've heard he also holds some children of people he does business with in Mexico, to make sure they don't double-cross him in business dealings. He's stowed these kids, three or four at most, at Street Business, and Jackie knows nothing about it. And when officials question what goes on at Street Business, Juan pays off whoever he needs to to keep Street Business above the law. This way Street Business always looks clean. Of course, it's all a lie, but he's got enough money to keep everyone involved quiet."

I sat back and contemplated what she said.

"Jackie is so sincere, and he looks up to Juan so much. He is blind to what Juan really is," she said. "I am very fond of Jackie. He's been so good to Slide."

"You mentioned torture and murder. Have you seen Juan actually harm someone?"

"No, it's just talk. But people who anger Juan sometimes disappear and are never seen again. It is never Juan who does this, of course. He always needs to be the good man. I think he has deluded himself into thinking that he really is a good guy. But he has others do his work for him. And he always arranges it in a way that cannot be traced to him, which allows him to maintain his charade as a good man."

"Is it just the stories you hear from the immigrant workers which make you believe Juan's a criminal?"

"That's one part of it," Carmen said. "But I have firsthand knowledge of some of his business dealings. Juan has a legitimate international trading and import business, but his real wealth comes from trafficking in drugs from Mexico. He launders the funds through his other businesses, and uses his money to buy status and respectability in Boston. But in truth he is little more than a drug dealer."

"So forgive me for being cynical," I said, "but it seems like you hit the jackpot with Juan. He may be a bad man, but I imagine being a kept woman on a horse farm in Weston beats where you were when you met him."

Carmen looked into her near-empty glass. I raised the bottle. She shook her head and stirred the remaining ice cubes with her finger.

"A whore is a whore, Spenser," she said, "no matter how expensive the clothes."

"So why don't you just leave?"

"I can take care of myself, Spenser," she said. "But I fear for the others, Martita and her baby, her brother. And for one in particular."

She drained the rest of the scotch from her glass.

"I don't have children, Spenser, and I doubt that I ever will. But when Slide showed up at the stables, I sort of adopted him. Juan is jealous of Slide because he senses I care more for a lost little boy who needs my love and help than I do for him," Carmen said. She thought for a moment. "I have not lived a true life, Spenser. I think Slide may have been brought into my life to open my eyes. I want to protect Slide. And I want to be the person

Slide believes me to be."

"And where do I fit in?"

"I want you to help me stop Juan Alvarez."

I swirled the ice in my glass, then set it down again.

"I currently have a client," I said. "Street Business. Jackie has asked for my help in eliminating a threat to its existence. Juan Alvarez is the principal support of Street Business, which you yourself acknowledge is a good place. Helping you bring down Juan Alvarez would seem to be a conflict."

"Unlike Street Business, I can pay you," she said.

"Not exactly the point," I said.

She nodded. "If it is possible to bring down Juan without harming

Street Business, will you help me?"
"I'd be a fool not to," I said.

15

Susan was giving pearl her afternoon homemade Christmas cookie. Because we were at Susan's house, homemade meant cookies from Rosie's Bakery in Inman Square.

"If we're not careful," she said, "Pearl will gain weight."

"Maybe 'we' could try to wean her off the cookies," I said.

"Never," Susan said. "I think you need to run with her longer."

"In that case," I said, "I think I deserve a cookie, too."

Susan brought a plate of Christmas cookies over to her coffee table. She sat down next to me on the sofa and rested her head on my shoulder.

"So do you believe Carmen?" she said.

"She has beautiful deep blue eyes."

"Martin Quirk has beautiful blue eyes. Do you believe everything he tells you?"

"Oddly enough, Quirk's eyes don't seem to affect me in the same way," I said.

"Hmm." Susan nibbled on a small corner of cookie. Her self-control was awe-inspiring.

"You are suspicious of the tennis player," I said.

"I am suspicious of all women who have beautiful blue eyes and athletes' bodies." She lifted her head up and took a sip of her chardonnay.

"Based on what I've told you, what's your professional opinion?"

"Impossible to say without seeing her in person. Not that I doubt what you've told me. But if what she's saying is true, the most fascinating subject in this whole drama is Juan Alvarez."

"How so?"

"Controlling, domineering personality. Needs to be loved and respected. Generous, devoted family patriarch. Yet also a vicious criminal."

"Sounds like Michael Corleone

in *The Godfather.*"

"Exactly," Susan said. "In the movie, his personality evolved, or devolved, over time. That's not always the case with dissociative disorders. But it is fascinating that a person can believe they are good, even when they are doing very bad things. They find a way to separate themselves from the bad, even when they are the direct cause."

"I sometimes forget you went to Harvard," I said. "I'm going to have to start writing the big words down."

"You don't need to write anything down," she said. "I'll just talk more slowly."

Pearl wandered over to the coffee table and snuffled around the plate of cookies. Susan shooed her away. Pearl ambled back over to the fireplace, circled around three times, and then sat heavily on the rug in front of the fire.

"So," I said, "based solely on what I've described, do you think Carmen is being truthful in her motivations?"

"Again, it's impossible to tell for sure without seeing her. So much is revealed by body language, by tone and inflection of speech. But yes, it's certainly possible she's telling the truth. She sounds like a fundamentally strong woman who has taken some pretty significant knocks. She enjoyed some hard-earned success in a tough, highly competitive environment, and then spiraled down lower than she ever imagined she could go."

"And now she wants to destroy the man who helped her back up?"

"Perhaps she's reached a point in her recovery where she doesn't need his support any longer, where she can stand on her own. She's now able to see him for what he truly is."

"And she couldn't before, because he was her savior."

"Yes. She needed to believe he was a good man just as much as he apparently does. It could also be that Slide is a trigger of sorts. For whatever reason, she's protective of him in a way she's never felt toward another human being, and that has caused her to see Alvarez in a different light."

"So do you think I should help her?"

"You've already agreed to help her. What I'm curious about is what you plan to do if your commitments conflict."

"You mean Jackie and Street Business."

"Yes," she said. "What if doing a good thing by bringing down Alvarez causes a bad thing to happen to a good cause?"

"Go with the greater good?"

"Is that the understanding you have with Jackie?"

"No, it's not."

"Then what?"

" 'First client wins' doesn't work, either."

"No."

"Then I guess I just need to make sure there's no conflict."

"Yes, you will."

We were silent for a moment.

"Shall I start dinner?" I said.

"Maybe we need to burn off those cookies first," Susan said.

I looked over at Pearl, who was curled up and sleeping in front of the fire.

"She doesn't look like she's ready for a run," I said.

"I'm sure we can agree on an alternative," Susan said.

"Might it involve seeing you na-ked?"

"Only if you keep your eyes open."

"Hot diggity." I held out my hand.

"Lay on, MacDuff!" I said.
And she did.

16

The light snow blew around in circles outside my office window. I was sharpening my powers of reasoning and analysis by reading comics in the *Globe* when Healy came in. He went to the coffeepot, poured himself a cup, added milk and sugar, and took a seat opposite my desk.

"Have some coffee," I said.

"Generous of you to offer," Healy said. He looked around. "Any bagels?"

Healy wore a light blue shirt and gray jacket with navy blue pants and a blue-and-red narrow striped tie.

I shook my head.

"What is that you're reading?" He stirred his coffee.

"Tank McNamara."

"Good to see you haven't lost the love of learning."

"I tried reading Aristotle," I said, "but the comics have better pictures."

"I'll keep that in mind," he said, "in case I ever learn to read." He eyed me over the rim of his mug.

"Thanks for dropping by," I said.

"You call, I spring into action," he said. "Although I was expecting bagels." He took another sip. "So

182

what's so confidential we couldn't have this conversation over the phone."

"I need some help," I said. "Do you know somebody named Juan Alvarez? Rich guy. Import/export business out of Boston. Big spread in Weston where he keeps his horses and illegal immigrants and probably some other stuff I don't know about yet."

"I've heard of him. Don't know him. Never arrested for anything that I can remember. I'll run his name. What's your interest?"

"I've got reason to believe he's running drugs and laundering money, perhaps as part of a Mexican drug cartel. He may also be involved in murder and human trafficking, including children."

"Sounds like a prince," Healy said.

I told Healy about Carmen and what she had relayed to me.

Healy leaned back in the chair. "She credible, this Carmen?"

"I think so."

"Maybe she had a fight with Alvarez, wants to teach him a lesson. Maybe she wants to take over his business once he's out of the picture."

I shook my head. "I don't read it that way. I believe her."

Healy gazed at me for a long moment. "That's good enough for me. Like I said, I'll run the file. What about these properties? Estate in Weston I understand. Legit business office in the Financial District. But the houses on Curtis Street. Fill me in."

I did.

"He owns the whole block?"

"All but one building, which he bought for his brother, who runs it as a shelter for runaways and street kids. Calls it Street Business."

"Think I've heard of it. Supposed to be okay. So what's the caveat?"

"Apparently Alvarez has covered himself pretty well, because any paper you've got on that place is a sham. Street Business isn't licensed. Probably a boatload of Child Protective Services violations, but it's serving a need and doing good work. I want to take down Alvarez and leave Street Business standing."

Healy shook his head. "Jesus, you don't ask much, do you, Spenser. And how, exactly, does a mere public servant like me fit in to your plans?"

"I need to find out what law enforcement knows about Alvarez and his business. I want to know who might have an interest in him — Feds, state, local — and for what. When I have that, I'll think up a way to smoke him out, something that sends him over the edge. If it works, Captain Healy of the Massachusetts State Police swoops in at just the right time and hauls him in."

"And his brother's illegal truant hostel somehow stands clear of the blast zone."

"Exactly," I said. "Shouldn't be too tough for a tough guy like you."

Healy exhaled loudly. "You're looking for a real fucking Christmas miracle."

"Courtesy of the Massachusetts State Police."

Healy stood up. "Look, let's take this in steps. I'll see what we've got on Alvarez, and whether there's any interest. If not, I'll forget I ever heard the name Street Business and head for the nearest wassail bowl. If there's something to go on, we'll move to step two. But best case, Alvarez goes down for something, we can't ignore an unlicensed kids' shelter in the middle of Boston. Something's got to change there. You might want to think about how to solve that part."

"I know," I said. "Alvarez goes down, the funding for Street Business vaporizes anyway. I didn't say it was a perfect plan."

"It isn't any plan yet," said Healy. He walked over to the sink and rinsed out his mug.

"I really should start going to Dunkin' Donuts for my coffee from now on, like a real cop," he said.

"You'd miss the stimulating conversation," I said.

"Yeah," he said. "Next time we can discuss *Garfield.*" He opened the door and left.

17

Healy called back the next morning.

"It's your lucky day," he said. "Turns out there's a great deal of interest in your friend Mr. Alvarez."

"From where?"

"The Feds have been looking at him for some time, for both drug and human trafficking. They're so eager they've actually requested our cooperation. Both Middlesex and Suffolk County DA's offices are in on it."

"And they haven't been able to nail him on anything?"

"No," Healy said. "He's apparently pretty slick. Covers his tracks well, and is well connected politically. Feeling is they may be running out of time."

"Why's that?"

"Those buildings you mentioned, downtown Boston? He just transferred title for all of them into a family trust. Prepaid his property taxes as well. Liquidated some other hard assets — stocks, bonds — into cash. And the word is that he moved out whoever or whatever has been in there around the same time."

"When was this?"

"About a month ago."

I thought for a moment. "About the time someone started hassling Street Business."

"Now, it could just be a co-incidence," Healy said. "He could just be doing some year-end tax planning. But it's also the kind of thing someone does when he's about to disappear for a while."

I considered the options. It could just be a coincidence, but thinking it was didn't get me anywhere. "Moving people out doesn't sound like tax planning. Any idea where the people or things got moved to?"

"No clue. There were eyes on the place, but apparently it's so deserted it was tough to get close without being noticed. Happened pretty quick, most likely at night."

"Raising cash sounds like he could be getting ready to bolt. Your sources have any thoughts on what he might be doing?"

"Not really, but could be he's preparing to flee the jurisdiction. Guy with his kind of money and connections could just drop off the grid."

"So now it's time for step two."

"Yes. Do you have a step two?"

"Not yet. It's in progress."

"I understand," said Healy, getting up. "You got hung up on *Garfield.*"

"Can't fool you," I said. "I'll call you when I've got a plan."

18

Carmen had given me her cell phone number. I called her.

"I have some questions for you," I said.

"I can't talk now," she said. Her voice was low and muffled. "Can you come out to Weston?"

"Yes," I said. "When?"

"How about six tomorrow morning? I'm staying at Martita's house. Our friend will be in Boston overnight and won't be back until late morning."

"Make sure you give the sentries a heads-up that I'm coming and that I'm friendly. Last time I visited, I almost got shot."

"I heard about that," Carmen said. "I think that guy is still looking for his rifle."

I was on the road to Weston at five-thirty the next morning. The sky was reddening past the tree line and by the time I got to the gates of the Alvarez compound the sun was up. The air was cold, the temperature in the twenties, and the snow was still white and unspoiled on the ground. I turned in to the driveway. The two granite lion heads on posts on either side had been decorated with Christmas wreaths of pine and cedar embellished with clumps of acorns and tied with big red velvet ribbons. I drove past the main house to the small cottage where Hawk and I had found Martita and her baby. I parked and went to the door. Before I could knock, Slide opened it. "Carmen said to bring you to the barn. She forgot to tell you she has an early tennis lesson." He was wearing his navy peacoat, but this time with a wool cap that came down over his ears.

He followed me to the car and got in the backseat. We drove slowly down a narrow lane to the big barn and parked alongside it. Slide led me through a small door to an office, which led into a huge open space. In the middle was a tennis court, where a man and a woman were playing. As we walked closer I could see that one of them was Carmen, in a pink sweatshirt over navy Under Armour tights, and she was playing a tall, thick-set man in dark gray sweats and a white T-shirt.

Slide and I sat in the bleachers and watched. Carmen served. She tossed the ball up with authority. Her racquet arm swung back, up, and over in a fluid arc. The ball landed on her opponent's back line before he had a chance to move. The man yelled, "Carmen, for crissake, this is a lesson, not the Open. Give me a break!"

"You'll never get better if I don't

push you, Sam," Carmen said. Her dark hair was pulled back into a single braid and tied with a pink ribbon.

She looked over at us. "Hey, guys. I'll be through in ten."

"Looking good," I said.

It was Sam's turn to serve, and he wasn't bad. Carmen swatted it back easily, and the ball landed at his feet where he couldn't return it. "Move your feet," she yelled at him. "Keep moving your feet."

After ten minutes Sam looked as though he might need a defibrillator. Carmen walked smartly off the court, draped a towel around her neck, shook hands with the hapless Sam, and joined us.

"Take no prisoners," I said.

"These rich guys don't feel they get their money's worth unless I make them suffer a little," she said and grinned. "How's my boy," she said to Slide, putting a hand on his cheek, and he beamed at her.

"You play real good," he said.

"For an old lady of twenty-nine, not bad. You play, Spenser?"

"Tennis is not part of my skill set," I said.

She laughed. "I wouldn't make you suffer. I like you. Slide, Spenser and I have some grown-up stuff to talk about. Would you go help Martita with the laundry and feed the baby? I'll see you later." Slide nodded, eyes wide, and took off.

"There's coffee. Want some?" Carmen said. I nodded and followed her to a small bar area. I poured myself a mug while she took a bottle of water from a fridge beneath the bar.

"A couple of things occurred to me after our last conversation," I said.

She smiled. "Of course. But couldn't you have asked me over the phone?"

"I like to see faces when I ask questions. What you say and how you say it are equally important to me." I could hear Susan's voice in my head. "Juan Alvarez is suspicious that I'm nosing around in his business. It occurred to me that he may be using you to find out how much I know, and to share what I know with you so that you can report it all back to him."

"You don't trust me," she said.

"In my business, that's what keeps you alive."

"So ask your questions."

"You told me you learned Juan is a drug dealer. Tell me how you found out."

She took a breath. "We were in bed. He liked to smoke this hash he brings back from Mexico. Strong stuff. Believe me, Spenser, I've been clean since rehab, but Juan says he needs it to relax." She looked at me, and I nodded. "He was feeling good, let me tell you. Then his cell phone rings and he takes the call. I can see his expression change as soon as he looks at the incoming number. He waves me away, so I go into the bathroom and close the door. But I can still hear him. He was talking to someone about a shipment coming through Juárez to El Paso. The distribution would take place immediately, and the money would be in his hands by the following week."

"It could be flowers," I said.

Carmen laughed, but it wasn't happy. "Yes, it could be flowers. Or shoes. Or tires."

"But you don't think so."

"One moment I was listening and the next he was inside the bathroom holding me by the arms and asking me why I was eavesdropping on his call. It happened in an instant. I told him the door was closed and that I couldn't hear a thing, but I don't think he believed me. He was very rough with me when we went back to bed. Once he fell asleep, I left." She took a sip from her water bottle. "Thank God he hasn't come near me since. Not in that way. I moved in with Martita two days ago. He is pleasant enough when others are around, but he's got his eye on me. He has me watched now whenever I leave the farm."

"How many guys does he have here? I'm assuming they're all armed."

"At least five. Will, the one who stopped you, and four others. One of them is Martita's brother. Marco. He's weak. I use him for bits of information."

"Do you have any reason to believe Juan is about to move away from here?"

She looked puzzled. "Move where? He travels a lot as it is. But we haven't said much to each other these last few days. I don't really know what he's thinking or doing."

"Let's say he were to disappear. Would he take you with him?"

"Before last week, I would have said yes. I thought he loved me and would take me wherever he goes. But I don't think that's true anymore. I saw his anger that night. I think he is more likely to have me killed than take me with him. He knows I know something. I'm a loose end. If he were to disappear, it would be because he is afraid.

And he's afraid of what I know and what I might say."

"So why hasn't he killed you already?"

"Because it's not that simple with Juan. He won't look like the bad guy. So he won't do the job himself. The killing must be arranged. He'll stage some kind of accident, with witnesses, to get himself off the hook. This way he can deny it, even to himself."

"In order to put Juan in jail, the authorities will need evidence that can be used in court. Would you be willing to testify against him at a trial?"

"Yes," Carmen said. "I would gladly say what I know. Others would as well."

"Really? These other people aren't afraid?"

"The guards and employees here, they fear Juan, but they aren't loyal. The guards are friendly and kind when Juan isn't around. But they would tell what they knew if it meant they could get away from Juan — or avoid prison."

"Do you have any idea where Juan keeps his business records?"

"I assume at his office in Boston? He does have a safe room here. It's underneath the stable, but the entrance is through a tunnel from the house. I've never been in there, but I know it exists."

"If something happened to Juan, what would you do?"

"I would survive," she said.

"You have any money saved?"

"Enough to last me awhile. I can always teach tennis at fancy resorts or tennis camps."

"Being independent is good. And what about Slide?" I said.

"Wherever I go, Slide goes."

"From now on, I want you to start checking in with me every couple of hours. I want to know you're okay," I said. "Any obvious opportunities for Juan to stage an accident in front of witnesses?"

"Juan is hosting another big charity Christmas party next week. It's a tennis-themed event, so I run it. I always get a few top players and other celebrities to come. It raises money for both the USTA and the USWTA, and Juan gets to show off to his rich friends. There'll be so many high-profile people here that day, I know I'll be safe."

"How do you figure you'll be safe? Just because it's a big crowd? Sounds dangerous."

"Too many people in a small space. Too many children. Too much publicity. If Juan wanted to stage something, I believe he'd choose a situation where he had more control."

"Anything else? Any other events between now and the end of the year?"

Carmen shook her head. "Not that I know of. Juan was planning to have a small dinner party on Christmas Eve, with just a few couples. That was before I moved out of the house. I assume the dinner has been canceled, or at least that I am no longer invited. Juan hasn't mentioned it since I left."

Carmen stopped and looked at me. "Spenser, I've answered all your questions. You've provided me with no information, nor have I asked you for any. I hope that you believe that I act on my own and not for Juan Alvarez, and that what I tell you is true." She waited to see if I'd reassure her. When I didn't, she went to her duffel bag.

"Would you do me a favor?" she said, handing me some hundred-dollar bills. "I want to give Slide a Christmas present. I don't own a car and don't want to ask Juan or his men to take me in to Boston to shop. I want Slide to have an electric-blue Razor. All the kids have them. You know, those motorized scooters."

"Consider it done," I said. "One last thing." I took out a small pad and pen and handed them to Carmen. "I need a map of the property. Just give me the general location of each building. And I need a map of the house. What's in each room, where the doors and windows are."

She talked while she drew the maps.

"Some setup, right?" she said. "The stable, this tennis facility . . ."

"I know ten guys out of work who'd be happy spending the night in one of the horse stalls if they're as grand as I think they are," I said.

"Not me. Horses scare me."

Carmen smiled. "A big handsome guy like you?"

She handed me back the notepad and pen.

"Hard to admit, but true."

We walked toward my car. "You'll make sure Slide gets my present? Even if something were to happen to me?" She looked at me, her hand held up to shield her eyes from the bright morning sun.

"I will. And I'll do my best to see that you give it to him yourself."

"Good. Take this, too." She handed me a piece of paper. "All my bank stuff. My accounts, my contact there. I want Slide to have it. I spoke to my dad and the bank when all this started with Juan, but there has been no time to make a new will. I know a written codicil is legal, and I have sent one to my dad and my lawyer. I know it is probably overly dramatic, but I want Slide to have something for his education, his future, if I were to meet with an accident . . . you understand." She stood very still.

"I do."

"Thanks, Spenser." She stood on the balls of her feet and gave me a kiss on my cheek.

"*Adiós,* Carmen." I got in my car and drove away.

19

I called Juan Alvarez and made an appointment to see him at his office, which was on Exchange Place on State Street. The building was a tall glass column with a black marble entrance. Inside the heavily gilt-painted lobby were the biggest potted palms I had ever seen outside the set of *Aida*. Over in one corner was a huge fir tree decorated with blue and silver balls for Christmas, which clashed with the brushed-gold elevator door.

I got off at the twenty-fourth floor. The elevator doors opened directly into a spare modern reception area. A young woman with strawberry-blond hair, brown eyes, and matching freckles sat behind a black granite workstation.

"I'm here to see Mr. Alvarez," I said.

"You must be Mr. Spenser?"

"I am," I said, flashing her what I hoped was a roguish grin.

She was not moved. "You're a bit late for your appointment. Mr. Alvarez doesn't like to be kept waiting."

So young. So jaded.

She got up and led me down a hallway and through a tall double door. Juan Alvarez got up from his half-crescent desk. "Spenser. Come in, come in." He waved me in. "Alice, what can we get for Spenser? Coffee, tea, or something stronger?"

He was wearing an expensive charcoal-gray bespoke suit with a faint chalk stripe and a floral Turnbull & Asser tie. His desk was burnished oak. On top of the desk were several neat piles of papers and three clocks showing different time zones.

"No, thanks," I said.

"Let me give you the nickel tour. I can't get enough of this view." He led me around the large room, which had a panoramic view of Boston Harbor and, on a particularly clear day, probably a good chunk of Newfoundland. The paintings on the walls reeked of expensive original. Picasso, Bacon, a Turner. Obviously not a discerning collector, but maybe it didn't matter when you had lots of money.

He waved me to one of the chairs opposite his desk, and we sat down. "Before you tell me why you are here, please allow me to apologize for my outburst the other day. I regret I came on a little strong. I have always been a very private man, and I find any intrusions into my affairs upsetting." He smiled.

I smiled. Amigos again. Just like that.

"Apology accepted, Juan," I said. "My innate curiosity isn't always understood or appreciated. Some people have told me I can be annoying."

He chuckled, but he didn't disagree.

I looked around. "This is a swell office," I said. "What type of business gets you the picture-postcard view?"

"I run an import/export business. Art, textiles, some clothing, small leather goods." He smiled some more, and I smiled back. After a moment, he said, "And to what do I owe the honor of your visit today?"

"I've been thinking of relocating my office, and I was wondering if any of those houses over by Jackie's Street Business are for sale. I'd even consider renting, if it got my foot in the door."

Alvarez smiled again. His teeth were white and even. *Maybe I'll ask for the name of his dentist, too.*

"An interesting concept," he said. "How many employees do you currently have?"

"One," I said, "including me. But I aspire to growth. And I have plenty of files."

Alvarez leaned back in his chair, put his arms on the armrests, and studied me.

"Your abiding interest in those properties intrigues and perplexes me, Spenser."

"And annoys?" I said.

"Amuses. Those buildings are simply investment properties, nothing more."

"I'm just a real estate junkie," I said. "I hate to miss a great investment opportunity."

"And an astute investor such as yourself would certainly check the public records, so you would know that I have recently transferred ownership of all of my Boston holdings. You would therefore know that I am no longer the legal owner of those buildings."

"Damn," I said. "Why unload such swell investments all of a sudden?"

"Not all of a sudden. It was the result of months of planning by my financial advisers. I hate to disappoint you, Spenser, but it was merely some long-overdue estate planning."

"I'm intrigued, Juan," I said. "Why the estate planning? Just contract a terminal disease? Plan to go skydiving? Recent unsettling visit from Marley's ghost, perhaps?"

Alvarez smiled. "Nothing like that. I am healthy and secure. But I do believe in looking ahead." He spread his arms and shrugged. "One never knows what the future might bring. It is best to be prepared."

"So if I'm stuck on that neighborhood, Jackie's place is the only one available?"

"Good luck with that, Spenser. Jackie should have sold that building long ago, but he is far too stubborn."

"Aren't you the number-one fan of Street Business? Don't you provide most of its support?"

Something dark clouded his face. Then it was gone.

"I am not a fan of Street Business. But I believe in supporting my family. That means I support Jackie. Funding Street Business is the manifestation of that support. But it is a financial black hole and an ill-conceived fantasy of a naive and foolish mind."

"So you wouldn't be saddened if it disappeared tomorrow?"

"I have done all I can to sustain Street Business. Jackie and my family know this. If it fails — when it fails — it will be through no fault of mine."

"Well," I said. "So much for my expansion plans. Thank you for your time, Juan."

Alvarez stood and followed me to the door. "A pleasure to see you, Spenser. I am reminded that I have yet to invite you and Dr. Silverman to my home in Weston. I will arrange that soon."

"I look forward to it," I said.

The receptionist was at her desk when I left Juan's office. She smiled. Perhaps I was getting to her.

"Leaving already?" she said. She looked disappointed.

" 'Promises to keep,' " I said. " 'And miles to go before I sleep.' "

20

Susan and I received an engraved invitation from Juan Alvarez to join him at his farm in Weston for the Sunday before Christmas.

The invitation was on thick, expensive card stock with a gold border and decorated with tasteful Christmas accents of wreaths and gold horns. According to the invitation, Juan Alvarez requested the presence of our company at a Christmas celebration at the barn. Drinks at noon. Brunch at twelve-thirty. Tennis at one. To benefit the USTA and the USWTA. There was a reply card where we could designate the amount we might donate, in increments of $5,000 per seat. Juan had slashed a line through the numbers and handwritten across the top, "Susan and Spenser, hope you will join us as my guests."

"Does that mean we get in free?" I said.

Susan had her head in my lap and was holding the invitation up to the light so we could both study it. "Each one of these must have cost twenty dollars," she said. She wore charcoal slacks and a form-fitting pewter blouse. A pewter jacket was thrown over the back of one of my chairs. She was transitioning out of her Dr. Silverman mode, but slowly.

"Ah, the tennis matches. When's the last time we enjoyed one of those?" I said.

"They're actually very entertaining, from what I understand," Susan said.

"Is there a part where they give away giant silver chalices to the winners?"

"Perhaps. I've never actually seen one in person, only on TV."

"I don't know about this," I said. "Carmen's brand of tennis scares me."

She raised her head from my lap and with the agility of a yogi turned it to look up at me. "Still overcoming a traumatic childhood tennis experience?"

"You should see her on the court. She doesn't fool around."

Susan sat up and took a sip of her pinot grigio, which had gone untouched on the table beside her. "No luck finding out who is causing Jackie his problems?"

"So far we know it's not the Catholic church. They gave up trying to buy the houses on that street months ago, after Alvarez turned them down on their last and best offer."

"And you think Jackie really cares about Street Business?"

"I do. But he appears to be the only one."

"Not Juan?"

I shook my head. "Juan funds it

out of a sense of familial obligation, but he doesn't like it. He's certain Street Business will ultimately fail, and he told me at least it won't be his fault."

"That's consistent with what Carmen has told you about Juan. He has to be the good guy. He doesn't want to be viewed as responsible for anything bad. He's certain it will fail, and he needs to not be responsible for its failure."

"True. But I think Juan has enough problems of his own right now without worrying about his little brother's social experiment. Despite that calm exterior, I think Juan is feeling the pressure and knows he could be seeing his empire start to crumble. My poking around isn't helping put him in a holiday mood, either."

"So why invite you to his home? 'Keep your friends close, and your enemies closer'?"

"If that were generally true in my business, I'd be invited to a lot more parties," I said. "But it's probably something like that. In any case, it's an opportunity to see more and learn more. But that goes both ways."

"What do you hope to learn?"

"I don't know. But knowing more is better than not knowing more. I just have to keep poking around until I find out something useful. I just hope I'm smart enough to recognize a clue when I step on one."

21

On Sunday we drove out to Weston. It was sunny, and the fresh snow gleamed across the meadows. I turned in at the Alvarez gates and continued on back to the barn, where there were already Porsche and Mercedes SUVs, a Bentley or two, and several Range Rovers. It was cold, 21 degrees, but the sun made it seem warmer.

Susan was dressed in black wool trousers and a cropped black leather jacket, and high-heeled black suede boots. I was wearing my gray wool slacks, a tweed jacket, and a dark gray turtleneck. Country Spenser.

We smiled at the other guests, and they smiled at us as we went into the barn.

A bar and tables and chairs were set up at either end. In the middle, wooden grandstands had been erected on either side of the tennis court. A string quartet dressed in Elizabethan attire was positioned in the front of the hayloft, playing Baroque music.

I nudged Susan and looked up. She followed my gaze, and we were silent.

"I don't mean to sound elitist," I said, "but wouldn't a jug band be more appropriate?"

"Or Garth Brooks," she said. "Maybe Juan doesn't know that 'country music' doesn't mean music from some other country."

"Or some other century."

She put her arm through mine, and we went toward the bar. To one side was the brunch table laden with large silver serving dishes and tureens waiting to be filled.

"Elegant," I said. When we reached the bar, I ordered a Grey Goose martini, and a sauvignon blanc for Susan.

"Actually, I'll have a Bloody Mary, very spicy, with extra lemon."

"Should I be concerned?"

"Extreme circumstances call for

extreme measures," she said. "This crowd is right out of WASP central casting. How did they let me in?"

"We're a forgiving people at Christmas," I said. "Just don't come back in January."

"Hello, you two," Juan Alvarez called out to us from beyond the bar. He walked toward us, resplendent in white tennis shorts, a white polo shirt with a monogram on the pocket, white Nikes, and a dangerous-looking black tennis racquet with a thick black handle. The country squire at play. If he couldn't hit a small white ball with that weapon, we were in for a long afternoon.

Juan leaned down and kissed Susan on each cheek and then

shook my hand. "Come with me. I'll make sure you get good seats," he said, leading us through the crowd. "Carmen does a wonderful job with these tennis matches."

Juan waved his arm in the direction of two center-court seats. "Enjoy. When you're ready, please go help yourself to the buffet. Now, if I may, I'll catch up with you later," he said, before heading in the direction of the local TV cameras set up at the other end of the barn. Their bright lights were clustered over a group of what I assumed were the celebrities Carmen had talked into participating in the event.

We could see Carmen coming through the crowd, trailed by a

man with a microphone and two cameramen. She was wearing white shorts that showed a pair of long, well-muscled legs, and a navy blue V-neck top. Her long, dark hair was pulled back in a ponytail and tied with red, white, and blue ribbon. She looked up into the stands, saw us, and after a quick word with the reporter, ran up the stairs, taking them two at a time. "Hello there! I'm so glad to see you." She gave Susan a kiss on the cheek and me an enthusiastic hug.

"I have to go warm up, but I wanted to say hi first. I really appreciate you coming out here for this." She nodded in my direction. "I'll bet you would rather do most anything else, wouldn't you?"

"I'm considering this a research trip," I said.

"Don't mind him," Susan said. "I'm looking forward to seeing what happens next."

"Hey, Carmen!" a young woman called from behind us. Carmen turned. "Kim!" They embraced. "You made it! How's the baby?"

"Fantastic! Hey, you look great. Retirement definitely agrees with you," Kim said.

"Kim, let me introduce you to my friends. Susan and Spenser, Kim Clijsters."

"Great to meet you," Kim said. "Carmen, I'm going to clean your clock today. Love you!"

"So that's what happens next," I said.

"No," Carmen said. "First mixed doubles. Two civilians, two pros. One set. Then one set of men's singles, then one set between Kim and me. Then we all go home."

"And how long do you think this orgy of tennis talent will take?"

"What do you think, Kim? Four, maybe five hours?" Carmen turned to Kim, who was laughing.

"I don't know how well you know Carmen, but she's a bad one. One hour, tops, unless we get into tie-breakers."

"All right, time to get ready. Head over and get some crab cakes before they're all gone," Carmen said. The two friends walked off, arm in arm.

"She's adorable," Susan said. "All that talent, and a dimple, too."

We made our way to the buffet table, where Susan put a small spoonful of vegetables and another of salad on her plate.

"Thanks for not showing me up," I said, helping myself to prime rib, mashed potatoes, and glazed baby carrots.

We took seats at a table as the mixed doubles got under way. Juan was partnered with a woman I thought was Martina Navratilova. Playing opposite them were John McEnroe and Rita Fiore. I noted Rita's white tennis costume, a fitted low-cut top and short pleated skirt, which showed off her spectacular legs. A little man sat atop the umpire's chair while a man in a tan uniform flipped big plastic numbers.

Slide had been pressed into service as one of the ball boys. He ran back and forth across the rear of the court, his face a mask of concentration. A young girl in pigtails worked the other side of the court.

"I had no idea Rita played tennis," Susan said.

"She's a woman of many talents," I said as I watched her smash a serve into the opposite court. Juan could only watch it go by.

"Forty love," the umpire called. Rita and John were winning. It didn't seem to be much of a contest.

We finished our meal and returned to our seats in the stands as the doubles were wrapping up. Rita and John had beaten Juan and Martina, though it had gone to a tiebreaker.

"I think now would be a good time to console Juan on his loss," I said to Susan. "Keep my seat warm."

Susan nodded. The crowd was loud and enthusiastic. I made my way through the throng to Juan. "Sorry about the match, but you put up a good fight," I said.

Juan smiled. "Playing with Martina is honor enough."

"You must be proud of Carmen for putting this all together. It's quite a party."

"She's really something, don't you think?" Juan said.

There was a tone of longing, perhaps, in his voice. As if he knew that he had lost her and he knew why and now his prize possession was soon to leave him. It didn't matter that he was the one to send her away permanently. Maybe he even loved her. *Pity me that the heart is slow to learn what the swift mind beholds at every turn.*

On my way back to my seat I went over to one of the dark-skinned men who were watching the match. "You Martita's brother?" I said.

He shook his head and pointed down the way to the next man standing guard. I walked over to him and stuck my hand out. "I'm Spencer. I took Martita and her baby to the health clinic last week, remember?"

The tall, heavyset man grinned at me, showing a lot of gold. *"Muchas gracias, señor."*

"Sorry, I only speak a little Spanish."

"I'm Marco. What can I do for you?" He kept his gaze on the tennis match while he was talking.

"I just wanted to say hello. Carmen tells me you're the security guard here. That's a pretty big responsibility, protecting all these people."

Marco grinned. "I am but one of many. Mr. Alvarez has . . ." He stopped to count. "He has ten guards here."

"But that's because it's a big

event today, right?"

Marco shook his head. "No, we are ten to twelve most of the time. Three shifts of four men. Sometimes more, sometimes less when Mr. Alvarez travels. But mostly ten to twelve."

"Good to know," I said. "I'm sure you are well trained."

"*Sí,*" he said, and his grin broadened. "And we are well armed."

"Did Carmen tell you I'm a private detective? I use a Beretta. Easy to handle, gets the job done."

"Smith and Wesson's a good weapon for close range. We have a snub-nose .38 special every time. Or for the ankle, a .25 Beretta." Marco was enthusiastic.

"Rifles?"

"For hunting. Not much for our work."

A burst of static sounded from Marco's right ear. I hadn't noticed his earpiece. Marco listened, then leaned into a microphone at his shoulder and said, "*Sí.* On my way.

"I have to go now," he said. "Nice speaking with you, Spenser. Thank you for helping Martita."

I went back to where Susan was sitting just in time to see Carmen and Kim take the court.

The umpire stepped forward for the coin toss to determine the first serve. Kim won the toss, and she and Carmen took their places.

Kim bounced in place at the baseline. She looked across the net at Carmen to make sure she was ready to start.

Her first serve whizzed over the net and hit the line.

Carmen watched it go by. She smiled at Kim and walked to the other side of the court. Kim served again. Another ace. No smile from Carmen this time. Athletes are all the same. Friendship gives way to the competitive spirit every time.

Carmen took the next two points, then Kim served two more aces and took the first game. It was Carmen's serve, and she made the most of it. Carmen rushed the net each time, ready to knock back every return. She won the second game without giving Kim a point. Sweat darkened the back of Carmen's navy-blue top. Kim's already pink cheeks grew pinker.

"Any chance we can leave without being noticed?" I said to Susan.

"So much for showing support," Susan said.

"I know what you mean, but just watching this has exhausted me."

Susan nodded. "Poor baby. We'll be discreet."

"Let's hit it, honey bun," I said.

And we did.

22

I was unlocking the door to my office when I saw a shadow in the corner by the stairwell. It moved. I backed up and reached for my weapon.

"Slide," I said. "What are you doing over there? Come on in." I opened the door.

He gave me a quick smile before putting out his hand. Maybe Carmen taught him. I took it, and gravely we shook.

"Are you very busy, Spenser?" he

said.

"Not too busy. Tell me what's up," I said.

Slide had on a new pair of jeans and a Red Sox sweatshirt, along with the same oversize navy pea-coat.

"I want to get a present for Carmen," he said. He looked at me, trusting that I would know exactly what the twenty-nine-year-old ex-mistress of a drug czar would fancy for Christmas.

"What's our budget?"

He looked worried. He dug into his jeans pocket and brought out some crumpled bills and gave them to me. Twenty-two dollars of hard-earned money. "This should do it," I said to him. "Follow me."

We left my office and headed toward the kiosks at Downtown Crossing, a street mall in an area near where Filene's Basement once welcomed tourists and shoppers from the suburbs. Now carts lined the center of the street, each one loaded with scarves, hats, ties, flowers, and cheap jewelry.

I moved purposefully ahead through the crowds of shoppers, Slide at my heels. The carts were draped with Christmas lights, and the holiday music blared from outdoor speakers.

I turned to check on Slide. His thin face was pale and drawn. I felt his hand reach out for mine, and together we went along, inspecting each cart for something that he

thought would be right for Carmen.

Slide tugged my hand when we
got to the jewelry cart. He picked
up a tiny silvertone pin in the shape
of a tennis racquet, edged with blue
enamel. "How much," I asked the
young woman behind the cart.
"Fifteen," she replied through a
thick wad of chewing gum.

"Can you gift-wrap this for us," I
said.

Slide's face showed a mixture of
happiness and relief to have found
the pin. He took the small box with
its glossy paper and bright ribbon,
and for the first time he seemed
unafraid of the crowd and the
noise. He held his hand out for his
change, and he shoved it and the

box into his jacket pocket.

"How about a hot chocolate?" I said.

He nodded, and we made our way through the shoppers to the Emack & Bolio's on State Street.

We sat at a café table, and I watched Slide enjoying the marshmallow on top of his hot chocolate. He mashed it with his spoon to make it last longer. It was serious work.

I remembered how my dad and uncles would take me for a treat at the drugstore. I could still taste the hot fudge that got chewy on the melting scoop of vanilla ice cream.

When we had finished, we stood on the sidewalk to say our goodbyes.

"Thanks for your help, Spenser," Slide said. "I think Carmen will really love this, don't you?"

"I do," I said. "How did you get in here from Weston?" I asked. "And how are you going to get home?"

"Got a ride from one of the men at the farm," Slide said. "They come in most days to run errands. Now I'll go over to Street Business. Either Joe or Frankie will give me a ride back."

I watched him melt into the crowd and disappear down the street. I wasn't sure how I felt about an eleven-year-old boy negotiating the city streets on his own. I know I had done it myself, once upon a time. I could almost hear

Hawk chiding me for being so soft. But that was different. It was Christmas in Boston. A boy should be able to travel these streets, as he had before. It was a time of peace and goodwill and all that. In a perfect world, the boy was heading for home, and parents watched for him at the window. Different times, indeed.

23

My red message light was blinking when I returned to my office. I looked at it for a moment and wondered if I could get a matching green light in the spirit of the holidays. Then I pushed the button. It was Healy. I called him back.

"Any news?" he said after answering.

"Happy holidays to you as well," I said.

"Right," he said. "Anything happening with Alvarez?"

"Well, Rita Fiore's got a mean serve."

"Very funny."

I told him about the tennis event at the farm.

"So what did you learn about Alvarez?"

"He's got twenty-four-hour security and a small but well-equipped arsenal out there. Carmen tells me he's got a safe room under the stable, which is probably where he keeps the kind of paperwork that can earn him the horizontal stripes. She doesn't think he's getting ready to bolt, but she also says she hasn't been close to him lately and wouldn't know."

"He wouldn't take her with him?"

"No. She thinks he'd kill her

instead because she knows too much."

"Well, I've got word the Feds are sure Alvarez is about to blow town. Definitely by New Year's, if not by Christmas."

"Christmas? That's two days away."

"There's a lot of chatter, lots of money moving around. People in motion," Healy said. "All circumstantial at the moment. But if we're going to nab him, it's going to have to be soon. Which means that if Alvarez thinks he has some loose ends to tie, he's going to act soon. You might want to let your friend Carmen know."

I hung up, then dialed Carmen.

"Spenser," she said. "I was just

about to call you."

"Are you okay?"

"Yes," she said. "But something is happening here. Do you remember the dinner party I told you about? It's still on, tonight instead of tomorrow. Juan just came by the stable to inform me. He was charming, but it was clear I was being instructed to attend, not invited."

"What time is this all transpiring?"

"Cocktails at six-thirty. Dinner at seven-thirty."

"Listen carefully, Carmen. The Feds believe Alvarez is about to disappear. If he means to do you harm, it will probably happen tonight. Right now you have two choices — run or stay. If you want to leave before the dinner, I'll drive out now and pick you up. If you want to stay, I'll bring some reinforcements with me and we'll watch what happens. Maybe we can catch Juan in something that justifies an arrest. But if you stay, you'll be putting yourself in danger."

"I'm not afraid." There was a pause. "Well, not much, anyway. I want to bring Juan to justice. My only concern right now is Slide. He's in Boston, at Street Business. I'll call Jackie and have him stay there tonight. If Slide's safe, I will stay."

I heard a low moan from the corridor. I looked up and saw a

shadow pass in front of the frosted window on my office door. There was a loud thud against the door, and the shadow disappeared.

"Carmen," I said, "I've got to go. I'll be out to Weston in about an hour. Call me if anything happens before then."

I put down the phone, slid open the desk drawer, and pulled out my gun. Then I walked over to the door, stood to the side, and listened. I heard what sounded like hoarse breathing in the corridor. I turned the knob, pulled open the door, and swung into the doorway in a modified Weaver stance.

Slide was sitting in a crumpled heap at my door. There was a deep cut on his forehead, starting just above his left eye. The eye was starting to swell, and the flesh around it already was starting to bruise. His nose was bloodied. By the way he was curled and holding his stomach, I could tell his ribs were bruised, if not broken.

I checked the corridor, then I squatted down next to him.

"Spenser," he said, his right eye open just a slit.

"It's okay, Slide. Don't try to move." I got down closer to his face. "You're going to be okay." He had been beaten, but nothing appeared to be broken. I scooped him up and carried him into the office and put him down on the sofa. Beneath the bulky peacoat, he was lighter than he should have been.

He shivered. I eased him out of the peacoat, then filled a basin with warm water. Using a clean cloth, I washed his face and hands as gently as I could, wiping away as much blood as possible. Other than the cut and the bloody nose, his head was fine, though the gash to the forehead caused a lot of bleeding. He'd have some bruises, and his body would be sore. I opened the first-aid kit I kept in my file cabinet and used gauze and tape to bandage his head. I thought he'd do okay without stitches.

I wrapped him in a blanket, and soon his shivering stopped. I made some hot tea at the boiling tap by my coffeepot and added four packets of sugar. I put a pillow behind his head and sat down next to him on the sofa, holding the mug out to him. "Come on, pal. This is good. Give it a try."

He did tentative sips at first, then drained the mug. Color returned to his cheeks. "Spenser," he said. "Jackie needs help."

"Easy, Slide," I said. "You all right to talk?"

He nodded.

"Tell me."

Slide tried to shift toward me and winced slightly. I moved off the sofa and squatted directly in front of him.

"They came for Jackie and beat him up." Very quietly, tears streaming down his face. "I think they may have killed him."

"Okay, little man, hang on. Tell me what happened. From the beginning."

"I go over to Street Business after I left you," he said. "When I get there, I see Joe and Frankie talking to two guys out on the street in front of the house. Then the two guys go inside, and Joe and Frankie walk away." He stopped and winced again. I filled the mug with water and helped him take a sip.

"Then what?"

"When I get inside, I see these guys yelling at Jackie. They're kicking and punching him, and one of them has got the iron poker thing from the fireplace, and he's whaling on Jackie. Jackie's trying to fight back, but he can't handle both of them."

"So what did you do?"

"I ran in and tried to help him. But one of the guys starts kicking and hitting me. When I break free, Jackie says, 'Get Spenser!' Even though they punched me in the face, I got away. I ran right here."

"What happened to Joe and Frankie?"

"They were there at first, but when the guys went into Street Business, they just disappeared."

"Was anyone else around? Any of the other kids? Any of the other staff?"

"Not that I could see. It was just these two guys and Jackie."

"Did you recognize the two guys? Had you seen them before?"

"No. Never."

"Think hard, Slide. Maybe at Street Business? Maybe at the farm?"

Slide shook his head. "No, I never seen them before. They were both big, with lots of muscle. Hispanic guys."

"Did you catch anything they said to Jackie?"

"No. They were shouting at him, but it wasn't in English. I didn't understand it."

"Okay, good job," I said. "You rest a minute. I need to make a phone call."

Slide's right eye grew wide, and he tried to stand up. "Please, Spenser, you've got to help Jackie. They hurt him bad."

"I will," I said. "Let's get you taken care of first."

I called Susan.

"Are you free right now?" I said. "I need your help." I filled her in on Slide and Jackie.

"Are you calling the police?" she said.

"No. I want to get over to Street Business first. Right now I need to make sure Slide gets checked out. Then I need to find Jackie." I looked at my watch. It was five past one. "And then I've got to get out to Weston. Alvarez may be on the move, and Carmen may be in danger." I looked over at Slide. He was staring at me intently, but he was quiet. "All that paperwork can wait."

"I'll meet you at Mass General," Susan said. "I'll take care of Slide. Just tell me Hawk will be with you."

"My next call," I said.

24

Hawk was at the Harbor Health Club. I updated him on developments. "Meet me at Mass General emergency," I said. "I think I want Vinnie in on this, too."

"I'll find him. Be there in fifteen minutes."

I bundled up Slide in the blanket and headed out the door.

"Okay, little man. Let's go get you fixed up. Then I'll find Jackie."

Susan, Hawk, and Vinnie Morris were waiting for me at the emergency entrance to Mass General. Hawk spoke with the triage nurse, who either knew him or wanted to know him, and she wheeled Slide inside, Susan at his side.

Hawk, Vinnie, and I drove over to Street Business in my car. On the way, I called Healy.

"The game's afoot," I said. I filled him in on the beatings. "If your sources are correct, and Alvarez is about to fly, tonight may be his opportunity to dispatch Carmen. Time for plan B."

"Which is?"

"Hawk, Vinnie Morris, and I scope out the dinner party. If something happens, we move in and stave off disaster until you and your guys can come in. Can you meet me in Weston at six?"

"Not much of a plan," Healy said.

"It's all in the execution. And it's all I got at the moment." I hung up.

All was quiet at Street Business when we pulled up. We walked up the front steps and banged our way through the front door.

Joe and Frankie were in the sitting room to the right of the front door. Joe was sitting in an overstuffed chair, and Frankie was lounging on the sofa. Each had a cigarette in one hand and a Budweiser tallboy in the other.

"Hey, what do you want?" Frankie said. Both of them started to get up.

I decided that of the two, Frankie might be more useful to us. I walked to Joe without saying a word, grabbed his face in my right hand, and pushed him back down into the chair. Hawk and Vinnie stood on either side of Frankie.

"You might want to sit," Hawk said to him. Frankie sat.

Joe struggled to stand up. I jabbed him on the nose with a quick right. Blood spurted as his hands went to his face. Beer splashed off the wood floor. He might have swallowed the cigarette. I grabbed him by the hair and yanked him over to Frankie's sofa.

"Hey! Hey! What the fuck?" Joe said.

I stepped around the sofa and kicked him in the stomach. Then I picked him up with both hands and slammed him against a bookcase. He staggered for a moment, then fell, pulling the bookcase down on top of him.

"I see the rules have changed," Hawk said.

I stood over Joe in a loose crouch. "A kid gets hurt," I said, "the rules are different."

We all turned to look at Frankie. He was squirming on the sofa, panic in his eyes.

"What do you want? What do you want?" He was almost screaming. "Don't hurt me. I didn't do nothing. I didn't hurt no kid."

"Where are the boys?" I said.

"Upstairs," Frankie said. "They're all locked in their rooms upstairs. They're okay. Nobody hurt 'em."

His voice was rising in pitch, his words tumbling out.

"Where's Jackie?"

"I don't know," Frankie said. "Honest to Christ, I don't know. They took him away. When Joe and me got here, he was gone."

I leaned in and slapped him across the face. He turned his head away. A trickle of blood formed on the side of his mouth.

"As you can probably surmise," I said, "I have very little time to deal with you, and even less patience. So you're going to tell us what happened here. You're going to be clear and concise and complete. You're going to tell us why you two geniuses let Jackie get beat up by a couple of thugs. You're going to tell us where Jackie is. And you're going to tell us why the residents of this safe house are locked in their rooms while you and Joe have a frat party down here. Got it?"

Frankie looked from me to Hawk to Vinnie. Hawk stared at him without emotion. Vinnie gazed outside the bay window out onto the street. Not a sympathetic audience. There was pure terror in Frankie's face.

"Okay, okay," he said. "It's like this. Joe and I get a call from Mr. Alvarez. He says some guys are coming by, he wants them to talk to Jackie. He tells us to let the guys in, then take a walk for an hour. So that's what we do. We let the guys in, and we get lost. When we get back, Jackie and the guys are gone.

Then Mr. Alvarez calls and tells us to lock up the kids and wait for his orders. So we do that. We lock up the kids that are home, and we wait down here for the ones who are out to come back. When they do, we grab them and lock them upstairs, too. Then you guys show up."

"Who were these guys? Men from the farm?"

Frankie shook his head. "No, not from the farm. Two big Hispanic guys I never seen before. Tattoos and shit. Scary guys."

"What did Alvarez want the guys to talk to Jackie about?"

"I don't know," said Frankie. "Honest to God, I don't know. He didn't say, and you don't ask Mr. Alvarez questions. You just do what

273

he tells you."

"You've been around here awhile. You have an educated guess what Mr. Alvarez would want them to talk with his brother about?"

Frankie rocked back and forth on the sofa. He shook his head from side to side. He swiveled his head to look at Joe. Then he looked back.

"Please, don't make me do this." Frankie was almost crying. "He'll have me killed."

"Who will?" I said. "Joey here? I don't think he's in any shape to do you much damage."

"No!" Frankie started to wail. "Mr. Alvarez. I talk about his business, he'll have me killed! Please!"

I slapped him twice to get his attention. "You don't tell us, and the three of us are going to drag you up to the roof and bounce you off the sidewalk."

"You don't know Mr. Alvarez." Frankie was pleading.

"You're afraid of Alvarez? Look around you, Frankie. Alvarez isn't here. We are. You might want to be more concerned about what we want."

Hawk grunted. Vinnie continued to stare out the window, as if the deserted street held more interest than the drama unfolding in the room around him.

Frankie burst into open tears. I waited. He cried. I grabbed the neck of his sweatshirt, twisted it in my hand, and lifted him up off the sofa.

"I'm waiting," I said softly. "But not much longer." I let go, and he dropped back.

Frankie looked back again at Joe, who hadn't stirred. Then he turned back to me and sniffed twice.

"Okay," he said. "Okay." He shook his head and gave a deep sigh.

"Mr. Alvarez hates Street Business. Wants to shut it down. It loses a ton of money, and he thinks someone will find out that it's here and it's not legal and the police will come, and Mr. Alvarez doesn't want that kind of attention. But he can't shut it down, because it's important to Jackie and Mr. Alvarez promised his mama he'd support Jackie and he can't go back on his promise. So he tries to buy Jackie out, but Jackie's proud of this place and thinks he's doing a good thing, and he says no. So then he tries to scare Jackie into giving up. He thinks Jackie is weak and will just give up if he's threatened, so Mr. Alvarez hires some guys to cause trouble. Nothing serious, you know? Just push some of the kids around, take some of their money. Just enough to frighten Jackie."

"But Jackie doesn't get frightened," I said.

"No," said Frankie. He shook his head again. "Jackie grows a backbone, just at the wrong time. He won't quit. He fights back. He asks Mr. Alvarez for more help, so Mr. Alvarez sends Joe and me to guard the place. And Jackie brings you in to make the threats stop."

"Not knowing that his brother is the one causing the threats. Not knowing his security guards are working for the enemy."

Frankie looked down and swallowed. He didn't say anything.

"When did Alvarez decide that Street Business was a problem, and might attract the wrong attention? When did he decide to shut it down? Funny he gets a conscience all of a sudden."

Frankie looked up at me, then shut his eyes tight, as though thinking caused him intense physical pain.

"I dunno," he said. "Maybe a month or so ago?"

"Okay," I said. "I'm going to ask you this just one more time. Where is Jackie now?"

Frankie recoiled and started to shake. Tears began running down his face.

"I told you, I don't know!" He was shouting, his voice hoarse and filled with fear. "I'd tell you if I knew. Honest to Christ, I would. But I don't. He just wasn't here when Joe and me got back."

I stood over him for a moment. He dropped his head and didn't say anything else. I looked at Hawk. Hawk shrugged.

"Vinnie," I said. "Will you entertain Frankie and Joe here while Hawk and I confer in the hall for a moment?"

Vinnie looked at Frankie without emotion.

"Sure," he said.

Hawk and I walked out to the hallway.

"What do you think?" I said.

"Think you scared him," Hawk said.

"Do you think he's holding back anything from us?"

"I think he's told us all he knows. Now what?"

I looked at my watch. It was almost three in the afternoon.

"We've got to get out to Weston. Time to call in the cavalry, I think."

25

I called Quirk, who wasn't in. I got transferred to Belson, who was.

"Frank, I need help."

I told him about Slide's beating and Jackie's disappearance, about Alvarez and the machinations surrounding Street Business.

"What I'm not hearing in all this, Spenser," he said, "is the magic word 'homicide.' That's what we do in this department. Why don't you just call for a patrol car to roll by and mop up your mess."

"I've got a missing person and possible homicide," I said. "And I need help from someone I trust. A patrol unit is going to call in Child Protective Services, and this place will get shut down. I need someone to stabilize and sit on the place for a few hours, until I get another piece of it resolved. I need time until I can figure out how to keep Street Business in business."

"So you need me to babysit a house filled with juvenile delin-quents while you figure out how to keep an essentially illegal business in play? We have real work to do, Spenser."

"I need to protect another client," I said. I gave him a brief summary of Carmen and Alvarez. I told him about Healy and the Fed and state investigations. "And so help me, Frank, if I need to shoot someone so you've got a homicide to get you down here, I'll do it."

Belson sighed. "Okay, Spenser."

I gave him the address.

"Curtis Street?" he said. "Is that by St. Bart's?"

"Yeah," I said. "It's a few blocks away."

"My kid sister knows the priest down there. Said the Mass at her wedding. I'm blanking on the name, but he seemed like a regular guy."

"Ahearn?" I said.

"Yeah, that could be it. Ahearn. They do a lot of work with kids at St. Bart's. I'll send a squad car down there, too."

Father Ahearn arrived at Street Business in about ten minutes, along with ten guys who had to be the world's most intimidating chapter of the Knights of Columbus. A patrol car pulled up, and Belson followed right behind in his unmarked Crown. Martin Quirk was with him.

"I called Marty," Belson said. "He's got more juice than I do."

Quirk was dressed in a navy-blue blazer with a light blue button-down shirt and bright red sweater vest and gray slacks. His red tie had a small Christmas-tree print. He looked clean-shaven and fresh as a spring morning.

"Left my grandkid's Christmas

pageant for this, Spenser," said Quirk. "Make it worth my time."

"Sorry, Marty. It's important."

Quirk nodded. "Frank filled me in." He nodded to Hawk and Vinnie. "We'll hold down the fort here. We never saw you. Now go."

We headed for Weston, Hawk riding shotgun and Vinnie in the backseat. We had just hit the Mass Pike when my cell phone rang. It was Susan.

"Spenser," she said. "We have a problem. Slide is missing."

26

"I was in the room while the doctor examined him," Susan said. "They had to take him for X-rays of his ribs to see if any were broken. They brought him back to the room and we waited. You know how it is. Emergency room. Holidays. Slide was pretty antsy, and I tried to distract him, but conversation with eleven-year-olds is not in my résumé."

"How did he get away?"

"After what seemed hours, but

was probably half an hour, the doctor came back with the X-rays and said there were no broken ribs. She gave Slide a couple of Tylenol to take before bedtime if he ached too much.

"She said he could get dressed and we could leave and he was a fortunate young man not to be more seriously hurt. I went into the bathroom for a moment, while Slide went behind the screen to get his pants and shirt on.

"When I came out, he was gone. In thirty seconds. I ran out in the hallway and looked up and down it. Not a sign of him."

"Any reason to think someone grabbed him?"

"No," Susan said. "There was no

one around in the hallway, and I ran out to the lobby and asked the desk nurse if she had seen Slide and she said yes she had and he had been alone. He had headed for the main exit. One good thing. He's fine except for some really deep bruises."

"Okay," I said. "He probably heard me say Carmen was in danger. I'll bet he's trying to work his way to Weston, same as we are. We'll look out for him. Don't worry."

"Easy for you to say," Susan said. "The road out there is not a place for a kid right now. I'm going to drive toward Weston and see if I can find him."

"He's a tough kid, Susan. I don't

want you mixed up in what's going on out here. He's found his way by himself out to Carmen a lot of times before. I'll call you the minute I can."

27

We caught up with Healy in the parking lot of a Bruegger's bagel shop on Center Street in Weston. He was in an unmarked state police cruiser, with the engine running. I pulled in to the space to his left. Hawk rolled down his window. The darkness had started to gather, but I could see someone sitting in the passenger seat next to Healy.

"Nice touch, picking a place with bagels," said Healy. He stared straight ahead. "Got some good news, Spenser. Boston PD located your friend Joachim Alvarez. Somebody dumped him at the emergency room at Beth Israel about an hour ago."

"And?"

"He's beaten up pretty bad. But he'll live."

"Well, that's something," I said. "Were you able to scare up any help for this operation?"

Healy snorted. "You wouldn't know by looking around, but there are about twenty pairs of federal and state eyes on us right now."

Healy looked over at his passenger. "This is Special Agent Goldberg of the FBI. He insisted on joining me, even though it could blow the cover off the entire fucking operation. He wants to make clear that this is a federal matter and he's in charge."

He stared straight ahead again. "Goldberg, the driver is Spenser. The other two guys don't exist and you never saw them. I miss anything?"

Goldberg cleared his throat. "Exigent circumstances, Spenser. We haven't had time to map this out precisely. We don't have a warrant. We'll need some reason to go on Alvarez's property."

"So there needs to be some emergency, some threat to human life."

"Exactly," said Goldberg. "We'll be waiting at several points just off the property line. Something happens, we need a pretext to go in. A gunshot, broken glass, loud shouts, something. We don't hear anything, you're on your own."

"Got it."

"Give him this." Goldberg handed Healy a small walkie-talkie. Healy passed to it Hawk.

"Worst case," Goldberg said. "Call us."

"Okay," I said. "But I won't be reporting in every five minutes. It stays off unless I turn it on. I don't want to be discovered because you feel the need to check on us at the wrong time."

"Spenser, we're improvising here. When you do that, a lot can go wrong in a hurry. The whole thing can turn to shit pretty quick. Do you understand?"

Healy sighed. "He understands, Goldberg. You pretty much just described his entire career."

Healy and Goldberg told us where the FBI and state troopers would be staging. It was quarter past six when we backed out of the parking lot and headed off to Alvarez's farm.

28

Heavy clouds concealed the moon. The thermometer inside the car read 18 degrees. Better out than in. Days-old snow banked the sides of the road.

We parked alongside the long driveway and extinguished the headlights.

"How do we play it?" Vinnie said.

"We sneak up to the house and wait," I said. "Watch for sentries and try to count the guns on-site tonight."

"You think the fireworks start right away?" Hawk said.

"No," I said. "He probably waits until dinner or after, when all the guests are settled and relaxed. If he needs to stage this to make it look like he's a victim, he needs this to be a nice, normal party, until it's not."

"Once it starts, how we gonna stop things from the outside?" Vinnie said. I looked at Vinnie in the rearview mirror. He was testing the action on his Glock.

"We wait until dinner. Cocktails will most likely be in the living room to the left of the front door. It has big picture windows on the front and side. A big archway leads from there into the dining room.

That has French doors to the deck on the back of the house. When the guests move to the dining room, Hawk and I go in and cover the archway and the door to the kitchen. Vinnie, you stay outside and cover the French doors. Keep your eyes on Carmen. Hawk and I will deal with anything else."

Vinnie nodded.

"And when something start to happen, we move in," said Hawk.

"Any idea what the something might be?" Vinnie said.

"No," I said. "My guess is a robbery. Healy thinks Alvarez will try to stage his own kidnapping — he disappears, and Carmen gets killed in the crossfire. All we think we know is that Alvarez needs to look like the victim."

"Think the guests are in on this?" Hawk said.

"Probably not all of them. Carmen said she doesn't know everyone invited, but some are social acquaintances Alvarez isn't particularly close to. He likely needs some authentic guests to sell this to the police afterward," I said.

I waited a moment. Then, "Game time."

I had switched off the overhead light. We left the car in darkness and walked back up the road along the tree line to the driveway.

Cars were arriving, mostly limousines, letting out women in furs and men in evening clothes. There was a man in livery opening the car doors and a butler opening and closing the large front door. The pillars were festooned with fir garlands, the door frame draped with boughs. A huge wreath with a red velvet bow was hung in the center.

From our vantage point on the driveway we were able to see the Great Hall each time the butler opened the door. A huge crystal chandelier hung from the ceiling, and the polished floor glowed.

"My, my," Hawk said. "How the rich folk live."

"So *Masterpiece Theatre*," I said.

"You did say handguns only," Vinnie asked.

"Yes. And no shooting if we can help it. We want to get Carmen out of there and leave Alvarez for the

Feds. No need to do more."

"And Slide, if he show up," said Hawk.

"There is that," I said.

We spread out and made our way to the house. No guards were visible. No more cars came. We could see the guests in a room to the left of the Great Hall, drinking their martinis. I looked at my watch. Ten after seven. I looked back up and saw that the room was emptying out and guests were headed for the dining room. Vinnie moved into position around the back of the house. Hawk and I stayed by the windows to the dining room and watched. The cold and the tension pressed sharply up against me.

The dining room was ornately

decorated, with a large oval table in the center. Sixteen guests were seated around it. The walls were covered with textured rose-colored fabric. There were two heavy silver candelabras on the table, each with eight candles. Each place was set with four crystal goblets, and tiers of silverware. Alvarez sat at one end of the table, resplendent in black tie and tails, flanked by two women with expensive faces talking animatedly across him. He was trying to look interested.

Carmen sat at the other end of the table. She glowed in an emerald-green gown, tastefully low cut. She wore diamond drop earrings that swung when she moved her head. There was no trace of the

Carmen I knew, the tomboy who bit her fingernails and served tennis balls like bullets. I watched her talk to the man on her right and then after a few minutes turn to the man on her left. She laughed at their jokes and talked to them with ease.

I looked at the guests at the table, remembering that they might not all be guests. Everyone looked prosperous and slightly dowdy, as befitting old Boston money. *Which one of these is not like the others,* I thought. My gaze picked up on a youngish couple near Carmen's end of the table. They were in their forties, and they definitely did not fit the mold. Maybe it was the designer clothes, his five-hundred-dollar haircut, and what appeared to be her inability to make conversation with the distinguished older man next to her. They had to be plants.

Hawk slid back to my side. I signaled him and wordlessly pointed out the faux guests. He nodded.

We waited. I could hear footsteps followed by low Spanish-speaking voices coming from the front of the house, and moved down the side of the house to take a look. There were five of them, wearing kerchiefs for masks. Three of them had rifles and two had pistols.

Hawk had moved up behind me.

"Some militia," Hawk muttered. "Deer hunting."

They trooped inside. We drew our guns and followed in behind them. They marched directly through the Great Hall and the parlor and into the dining room, and pointed their weapons at the stunned and by this time tipsy guests. We stayed back, at the edge of the parlor, waiting for Vinnie to appear outside the French doors on the other side of the dining room.

One of the women guests giggled. One of the intruders walked over and slapped her across the face. She screamed. The rest of the guests froze, and the room fell silent. Two of the men held canvas bags and went from guest to guest demanding money and jewelry. Everyone complied except Alvarez.

He stood and bellowed, "Who are you? Stop this immediately!" His protests had the air of summer-stock theater.

I saw movement outside and hoped it was Vinnie. Another woman screamed as one of the masked men yanked off her necklace. Just then two men dressed like restaurant captains appeared in the entry with guns. "Drop your weapons," they shouted at the robbers. The men with the rifles threw their weapons on the floor, while the two with pistols stood motionless on either side of the archway.

"Here we go," Hawk said. He stepped through the archway and put his gun against the neck of the closest gunman. I darted back out to the Great Hall and into the kitchen. The kitchen staff was busy preparing plates when I entered. I put my finger to my lips and waved my gun at them. They froze. I pushed through the door to the dining room just as Vinnie kicked in the French doors and entered, his Glock drawn. The guests were silent with terror. Hawk had moved with his man along the side of the wall, facing the table and the windows and with a clear view of the archway. "Everyone drop their guns or we shoot. Your choice," I said. The guards were holding their guns on the masked men as well.

Alvarez was trembling. He looked baffled.

"Spenser? What in the world is

this?"

For a moment, the air was tight and nothing happened. And then everything happened at once.

One of the restaurant captains raised his pistol and pointed it at Carmen. Vinnie turned and shot him in the chest. The captain crumpled to the floor in front of Alvarez. The man I had pegged as a plant reached under the tablecloth. I saw the glitter of the candlelight on his gun as he trained it on Carmen.

"Carmen!" Slide appeared in the archway and let out a piercing scream.

Before I could shoot, Carmen grabbed a knife from the table and flicked it at the seated assassin. It struck his chest and sent him toppling backward.

The other captain lowered into a crouch and fired at Slide. Hawk pushed his prisoner into the gunman on the other side of the archway, grabbed Slide and yanked him to the floor. Hawk pulled Slide toward him and covered him with his body.

Vinnie shot the second captain in the face, then swung his weapon toward the two gunmen heaped at the right of the archway.

Alvarez reached for the gun dropped by the first captain. I put my foot on the gun and my .44 against his forehead.

"I'll say this for you, Juan," I said. "You throw a hell of a party."

In a moment the room was swarming with state police and guys in flak jackets with automatic weapons. Healy walked through the kitchen.

"Nice of you to finally show up," I said.

"We came in as soon as we heard the scream," he said. "It sounded like you." He looked around.

"Good thing we got here before you shot everybody. Nice to have some witnesses survive, in case we want to bring someone to trial."

Slide had scrambled over to Carmen, who held him in a tight hug. Hawk stood as Healy and I approached.

In a single move, Healy palmed Hawk's gun from the floor. His voice was low and even when he spoke.

"You hit anyone with this?" he said to Hawk.

Hawk shook his head. "Don't think so."

Healy continued to look at Hawk, but his next question was for me.

"I assume you've got a permit for your piece?"

"You know I do," I said. "Do you want to see it."

"No," Healy said. He scratched at his chin.

"Kind of foolish of you, Spenser," he said, "to let this man walk into a situation like this without a weapon." He handed me Hawk's gun. I dropped it in my pocket. "I'm going to have to put that in my report."

He nodded at Hawk. Hawk nodded back. Healy turned and walked away.

We surveyed the room. The surviving gunmen were being handcuffed, and stretchers were being brought in for the less fortunate. The guests were being questioned, and the bags of loot were being examined and inventoried. A female trooper was speaking with Carmen and Slide, who continued to cling to each other. Healy and a group of men in suits and FBI flak jackets were gathered around a handcuffed Alvarez, who was staring at the chandelier above the table.

Vinnie had vanished.

29

I snuck out of bed at five a.m. Christmas morning, careful not to disturb Susan or Pearl. Susan stirred, briefly, and Pearl's eyes opened. "Shhhhh," I whispered to her as I got up. She followed.

It was dark out. Pearl and I walked once around the block, while the oven heated to 300 degrees. The air was crisp, and the day promised to be clear and sunny. "Fa la la la," I said to Pearl. She stopped to sniff something irresistible by a tree trunk before I was able to lure her back inside for her special Christmas breakfast of scrambled egg and cheese.

I opened the refrigerator and removed the turkey, the duck, and the chicken, which if all went according to plan would be transformed into turducken.

Susan and Hawk and I would be joined by Carmen and Slide. We had invited Vinnie but he had declined. I looked at the birds, whose appearance on the counter struck me as somewhat forlorn. I had never made this dish before, but I would persevere. The kitchen clock read five-forty-five. Dinner was at two p.m. The turducken should go into the oven at nine a.m. I had one

Christmas Day visit to make, and the timing was tight. I said to Pearl, "Why don't you make yourself useful? I'll take the turkey, you take the duck." She yawned and went to the sofa for her post-breakfast nap.

I got out the metal skewers and the big roasting pan. I made the herb mixture of butter, garlic, sage, and thyme. Then I spread the mixture between the skin and the turkey breast meat, and repeated this with the duck and the chicken.

I made two different stuffings, the turkey getting a mixture of cornbread, pork sausage, chopped onion, celery, olive oil, kosher salt, and fresh ground pepper.

The duck stuffing was made up of fresh and dried cranberries, orange peel, and French bread cubes. The chicken got more of the cornbread stuffing. I skewered the back of the duck closed and the back of the chicken. Then I brought the sides of the duck up to cover the chicken and skewered it closed and repeated it with the turkey. I felt vaguely as if I were on *ER*.

I turned the turducken over so the breast side was up and removed all the skewers except the one holding the turkey together.

I checked the clock. Seven-thirty. Susan had set her alarm for eight-thirty and had promised to put the monster in the oven at nine. I took a quick shower, shaved, put on some jeans and a heavy sweater and my parka.

I got in my car and drove to St. Bart's. Father Ahearn was sched- uled to say a ten a.m. Mass. Inside the church, I caught sight of him near the altar.

He saw me and smiled. "Merry Christmas, Spenser," he said in a low voice. "Thank you for coming."

"Merry Christmas, Father. Thank you for helping Jackie Alvarez and Street Business."

He nodded and led me to the side of the altar, where we couldn't be seen from the pews.

"So you have heard."

"Yes, Father. It sounds like a perfect solution. I wouldn't have thought it possible."

"The Lord works in mysterious ways, Spenser." He smiled. "The archdiocese of Boston, and this parish in particular, have a strong reputation in the area of social justice, and a close relationship with the city of Boston. The city is happy to have us take over the work of Street Business, and we are blessed to do so. And we pray for Mr. Alvarez's swift recovery. When he is healthy, there will be a place for him in our ministry." His eyes twinkled. "Who knows," he said. "We may yet have many buildings to manage in that neighborhood."

We had reached the massive door.

"So, Spenser, will we see you at Christmas Mass this morning?"

"I am afraid not, Father. But believe me, I will be giving thanks."

"And we will be praying for you.

317

And we will be praying for Juan Alvarez and his family as well. We are all God's children, regardless of our faith or our deeds."

" 'Those I fight I do not hate; those I guard I do not love,' " I said.

" 'And say my glory was I had such friends,' " Father Ahearn said, and we walked together toward the front of the church. People were beginning to drift in. "I see you are a Yeats man, too."

"My father gave me a book of his poetry when I was a boy," I said.

Father Ahearn shook my hand. "Merry Christmas, Spenser. May God be with you."

"And also with you, Father." I

said. Some things you just didn't forget.

30

Susan had set the table, and it was worthy of a spread in *Architectural Digest.* First an antique white linen tablecloth, then tall, delicate red wine goblets from a Venetian glass-blower. Green linen napkins, big ones, enough to withstand the rigors of the turducken mess, or whatever Pearl didn't get to first. The silver place settings, the pattern elegant in its simplicity, gleamed.

I poured champagne for all but Slide, who was having orange juice with a big maraschino cherry. We sat in a circle. Carmen and Susan were on the sofa, with Pearl between them. The women were admiring the pin Slide had given Carmen. I sat in an armchair opposite them, Slide on a footstool inspecting the blue Razor that Carmen had given him, and Hawk was in the loveseat opposite me.

I had finished the sweet potatoes, the brussels sprouts with walnuts, and savoy cabbage. The gravy was made. The turducken had come out of the oven and was loosely tented with aluminum foil, waiting for its half-hour before it had rested enough to carve. Pearl's gaze had not wavered.

Paul had called just before we sat

down, and Susan and I took turns talking with him. We would visit him in January, after the debris was cleared from Times Square.

Carmen and Susan were doing most of the talking. Hawk and I were content to look and listen.

"Hawk," Susan said, "do you have a special holiday tradition, other than spending the day with Spenser and me?"

"Celtics–Lakers game on at four," he said. "Thought I'd ask if I could watch it here."

Susan pointed at me. "He seems to know how to get sports on my television."

Hawk smiled. "I know that's not the only reason he come over here. Never understood the reason why you let him in."

"So what do you think Vinnie is doing on Christmas."

"Vinnie doing the same thing Vinnie do every day," Hawk said. "Get up, have breakfast. Go practice shooting, have lunch. Go shoot somebody or drink coffee all afternoon. Have dinner, buy some tail, go home and go to sleep."

Silence filled the room.

"What a delightful Christmas story," Susan said. "Thank you, Hawk."

" 'Course." Hawk smiled. "You did ask."

She lifted her glass to me, and then included all of us. "I think it's time for a toast. Merry Christmas to all, and how lucky we are to spend it together."

The dinner was a great success. I carved, and Susan served. The turducken was the center of attention. "Wow!" said Slide, on seeing the layers of turkey, duck, and chicken with stuffing between. "That's cool!"

"An engineering masterpiece," Susan said. Carmen raised her glass of champagne. "Are we lucky, or what?"

Hawk took a forkful and said, "I got to admit, I feel sorry for all those folks out there with their little bitty one-bird dinners."

I dropped a bite on the floor with furtive dexterity so that Pearl could partake. The faces around the table were a little different this year. And that was good.

After dinner, Susan started to clear the table.

"Leave those," I said. "Hawk and I will take care of the dishes."

"In that case," Susan said, "I think I'll have a quick lie-down. Watching you cook is exhausting."

I promised to call her in an hour. Hawk, Carmen, Slide, and I formed a pretty efficient kitchen crew. The dishes were washed and put away, and the kitchen was as spotless as if we'd never been there.

"I think Slide needs to run around outside a little," Carmen said. "It's not good for a boy to be stuck inside all day."

"There's too much snow to use

the Razor," I said. "I think there's an old basketball in the closet. There's a hoop up on the garage door. I brought it over here once to fool myself into thinking I'd get some exercise. You two can practice."

"I love a challenge." Carmen grinned.

"You going to come, too, Hawk?" Slide asked.

"No," he said. "Game's about to start. Plus, playing in the snow's bad for my image."

Slide and Carmen bundled up against the cold. I rummaged around the closet and found the basketball. We went outside, and Slide started running, tossing it up at the hoop, hitting the rim, the ball falling back into the snowdrift. He ran, picked it up, and tried again.

Carmen and I watched Slide. I said, "You serve a table knife with amazing power. You're good."

"Thanks. That's years of practice. We were so poor back in Puerto Rico, my dad gave me anything handy to practice my serve with. He'd have me toss 'em up in the air over and over again. Then get my racquet back and swing using my wrist." She paused. "He taught me to defend myself, too. I guess the other night the two came together. Instinct. I saw that gun and grabbed whatever was handy and used everything I had ever learned about speed, accuracy, and power." She looked up at me. "Lucky, right?"

"Maybe you were lucky he was a slow draw. I'd say it had more to do with courage and talent than luck. Now that you are free of Juan, what are you going to do?" I smiled at her. "You don't have to look for trouble."

"I thought I might help Jackie at Street Business. And take Slide to live with me. We both need to go back to school." She smiled at me.

I gave her a kiss on the cheek. "Merry Christmas, sport."

I left them and went back inside.

Hawk was standing by the window in Susan's living room, watching Slide and Carmen play in the front yard. The NBA pregame show was on the television. Stuart Scott was bantering with Mike Tirico in Los Angeles.

"Well," I said, "another successful Spenser family Christmas."

"Look like the family gets a little bigger this year," Hawk said.

"Perhaps," I said. Hawk continued staring out the window.

"Trying to memorize the recipe for turducken?"

Hawk shook his head.

"Thinkin' 'bout them," he said.

"What about them?"

"What we did."

I considered that for a moment.

"We went in there knowing we had to protect Carmen and Slide."

"Uh-huh."

"Right. Protecting a woman and a little boy. What in the world were you thinking?" I was trying to make a joke, but Hawk had gone somewhere else.

"Wasn't thinking," he said. "You know how it is. Situation like that, you don't think, you just act."

"And it bothers you that your instinct was to protect a kid."

Hawk stared out the window, his eyes fixed beyond Linnaean Street and out to the horizon. I had a feeling wherever he was looking, he was seeing himself at age eleven, a scared kid alone on the streets at Christmas.

"Not who I am, Spenser," he said. "That be you. Can't be you. Can't do what I do, thinking 'bout somebody else."

"You and I go in," I said, "I know

you got my back."

"I got your back, you got mine."
Hawk shook his head. "This feels
different."

"You kept Slide from being hurt,"
I said. "It doesn't mean you have
to adopt him. He and Carmen
don't expect a thing from you."

"Feel responsible for him somehow. And I can't do that. Can't be
responsible for no one but me."

"You do what you can do."

"And what's that?"

"You saved his life. That's probably enough."

We looked out at Slide. He was
terrorizing squirrels, throwing
snowballs at them in the now-bare
maple tree in Susan's front yard.

"I'll be checking on him," I said.

"Maybe go down to Street Business and show those kids how to box. You can join me or not."

Hawk exhaled and walked back to the sofa. Pearl ambled over and jumped up beside him.

"You did a good thing, Hawk," I said. "And that's enough."

He nodded.

I looked out the window. Carmen and Slide were laughing in the fading light.

"Merry Christmas, Hawk," I said.

"*Amani,* Spenser," Hawk said. "Peace."

When I left the room, Hawk had his head tilted back on the sofa and his legs extended on the coffee table. Pearl had stretched out and lay with her front paws and head in his lap. He patted her softly with his free hand while he watched the game.

31

I went to Susan's bedroom to wake her. For a moment I just watched her from the doorway. Even in repose, the sight of her always struck me like electricity. In all our years together, that had never changed.

She stirred.

"Where are our guests?"

I told her about the basketball, and the snowball fight, and gave her the score of the game.

"And Pearl?"

"Pearl's watching Hawk, in case he starts rooting for the Lakers," I said.

She smiled and sat up. She was still wearing her red Christmas dress. I sat down next to her on the bed.

"Have you come to unwrap your present?"

"I have," I said. "And perhaps ignite some holiday fireworks."

Susan pursed her lips.

"Fireworks sounds more like New Year's," she said. "I was contemplating something more reverent and sacred."

" 'O Holy Night'?" I said.

Susan smiled.

"That's the spirit," she said. She leaned forward and kissed me lightly on the lips. Then she pulled back slightly and met my gaze. A playful smile was on her face, and her eyes were brightly shining.

AUTHOR'S NOTE

There are people in your life, if you are very fortunate, who bring along with them untold gifts of laughter, love, and wisdom. Joan and Bob Parker entered my life in 1978, when they came to my New York office (then in my apartment because I couldn't afford a real office) to audition me to become, if I passed muster, Bob's literary agent. That day we formed a three-way friendship that gave me those gifts and much more.

Very soon after Bob's death, Joan and I were talking on the phone, trying to maintain our avoidance of anything approaching sentimentality or the maudlin, still suffering from shock at the suddenness of Bob's departure and our shared and separate grief, and Joan brought up that the morning he died he had been working on the Christmas Spenser. "I wonder what will happen to it now?"

Without thinking, I heard myself say, "Maybe I should try to finish it. Could I? Should I? What do you think?"

"I can't think of a reason not to

try. Bob would want you to," Joan said. "Go for it!"

And I did.

ABOUT THE AUTHORS

Robert B. Parker was the author of seventy books, including the legendary Spenser detective series, the novels featuring Jesse Stone, and the acclaimed Virgil Cole/Everett Hitch westerns, as well as the Sunny Randall novels. Winner of the Mystery Writers of America Grand Master Award and long considered the undisputed dean of American crime fiction, he died in January 2010.

Helen Brann is the Literary Executor for the Robert B. Parker Estate, and was Robert B. Parker's literary agent for thirty-two years, from 1978 to 2010. She is the owner of The Helen Brann Agency, Inc., which she founded in 1973.

The employees of Thorndike Press hope you have enjoyed this Large Print book. All our Thorndike, Wheeler, and Kennebec Large Print titles are designed for easy reading, and all our books are made to last. Other Thorndike Press Large Print books are available at your library, through selected bookstores, or directly from us.

For information about titles, please call:
  (800) 223-1244

or visit our Web site at:
  http://gale.cengage.com/thorndike

To share your comments, please write:
  Publisher
  Thorndike Press
  10 Water St., Suite 310
  Waterville, ME 04901